TALES WITH A TWIST

Tales With a Twist

A Collection of Short Stories

Mark Huenemann

CONTENTS

Some years ago, my spouse allowed me to sequester myself in my office for innumerable hours as I was wrote and edited the manuscript for a book. Not only that, but she willingly proofread the manuscript more than once.

And now she has done it again. Many thanks! And if some errors, slipped through, they are mine.

1

THE ARTIST

If you are not involved in the world of modern art, it is possible you may be unfamiliar with the work of the painter known as Chudzik. In fact, if you are beyond even the periphery of the modern art world, it is conceivable you do not even recognize the name. However, be assured that among those knowledgeable in the field of the visual arts, Rudolph Chudzik is among the most recognized and admired of any contemporary artist. His work is diverse and original, and critics and collectors alike describe his paintings in a continuous outpouring of highly laudatory terms. One could, in fact, assert that no living artist has a higher standing among connoisseurs of non-representational art.

Chudzik's ascension to the pinnacle of the art world followed an unusual path. He was born in England shortly after World War II of parents who had left Poland in 1938. His father became a highly successful businessman with an interest in politics and served two terms in the House of Commons. At an early age, Rudolph demonstrated talent in music, art, and maths. He showed exceptional promise in art and in mathematics and, at an appropriate age, through a combination of intellect and his father's influence, obtained admittance to

Oxford as a mathematics major. However, it was soon evident that he preferred the elective courses in art to those in his primary field of study.

During his second year at university, an incident involving one of Rudolph's math professors changed the trajectory of his education. Students in the professor's class were required to keep notebooks containing detailed calculations and formulas, and to periodically submit them to the professor for his review. Once, when the professor had finished reviewing Rudolph's work, he called the young man to his office. Unsure of the reason for their visit, Rudolph approached the professor's office feeling apprehensive. He knocked, a voice called for him to enter, and he was soon seated opposite the professor.

The professor began the conversation. "Chudzik," the man said, "the calculations in your book are, as usual, quite correct. Your ability in mathematics is more than adequate to earn your degree." Rudolph, feeling relieved, replied, "Thank you, sir." The professor nodded and continued. "However," he said, "I am intending to recommend to the dean that you be removed from the role of Oxford students in applied mathematics. In fact, my suggestion is that you be advised to cease your study of mathematics." Rudolph felt his mouth open, but no words came out. He was in a complete state of shock and disbelief.

Before the young student could collect his thoughts, the professor continued. "After I reviewed the calculations in the forepart of your notebook," he said, "I noticed the rest of the book appeared to have been used, as well." Rudolph, still in a fog of disbelief, remembered that he often used the rear portion of the book for sketches and drawings. "Mr. Chudzik," the professor said, "as I am not an expert in art, I took the liberty of showing your work to one of the senior members of the art faculty. It is on his advice that I suggest you give up mathematics in favor of the study of art, and I have taken the liberty of arranging an appointment for you with Professor Fossbaum. He will be expecting you at his office within the hour. I look forward to hearing of your decision." The math professor stood, shook Rudolph's hand, and ushered him out of his office.

It took Rudolph several minutes to digest the information he had just been given. He walked slowly across the quadrangle, his mind filled with questions. Why had he used his maths notebook to practice drawing? Why had his professor snooped in the notebook? What made the professor think it was within his purview to interfere with Rudolph's academic plans? How would his father react if told that Rudolph had spent two years studying maths at Oxford only to change to the study of art? What was the purpose of his appointment with Professor Fossbaum?

The name Fossbaum was not unknown to Rudolph Chudzik. Some of his elective courses in art were attended by art majors who talked about Professor Fossbaum and his reputation as a perfectionist and a hard taskmaster. He reportedly was harshly critical of his students' work and almost universally disliked by them. When out of his hearing, his students often referred to the man as "Professor Fussy Bomb." Understandably, it was with some trepidation that Rudolph found his way across the campus to the art faculty offices. He entered the building, consulted a directory, and climbed the stairs to the third floor. He found office number 312, took a deep breath, and knocked softly on the door. A strong male voice barked out, "Come!"

Rudolph opened the door and stepped into the office. Behind the desk stood a tall, thin man with long arms and large hands. He had black hair combed straight back, dark bushy eyebrows, and a prominent nose slightly angled to the left. He extended his right hand toward Rudolph and asked loudly, "Chudzik the amateur artist, I take it?" Rudolph nodded and felt his hand disappear into the professor's. "Sit!" the professor commanded, motioning to a chair in front of the desk. Rudolph did as he was told; the professor remained standing.

Rudolph had scarcely taken his seat when Professor Fossbaum turned to look out the window of his office. "So," the professor said, "You've been across there studying mathematics and dabbling in art, and your maths professor sends you to me. Why?" The man turned back toward Rudolph. He was not smiling. Rudolph cleared his throat and said, "Well, sir, he apparently sees some potential in my drawings. And I believe he said you do, also." The art professor's face wore a deep frown, which Rudolph began to think might be the man's normal expression. The man sat down behind the desk. A full minute passed as he looked intently at Rudolph, saying nothing, and stroking his chin with an outsized hand.

The professor suddenly turned back toward the window, and as if speaking to it rather than to Rudolph, said, "Potential, yes. Preparation, no. Study art? Definitely. Here at Oxford? No." Then the man paused. Rudolph, uncertain whether he was expected to say anything, waited. The professor, still speaking to the window, said, "Your potential must be developed. But you are not Oxford material." Rudolph was confused. He sat up straighter in his chair and said, "But I am already Oxford ... material." The professor nodded. "In maths, yes," he said. "In art, no. Oxford's art program is not only top rated – I say nearly the same level as the Royal College of Art – but also oversubscribed." Rudolph had no idea where the conversation was headed. The professor finally sat down and faced the student. When he spoke, his tone was less strident than it had been.

"Chin up, Chudzik," he said. "Once each term I choose a student who is lacking adequate training. I'm choosing you. I will personally work with you thrice weekly throughout the next term. At the end of that time, you will apply to – and due to my tutelage, be accepted by -- the University of the Arts in London. You will complete your studies there, then I will arrange for you to study in Paris. You will apply yourself with the utmost diligence, and we will see a capable artist emerge from that boring shell of a maths student."

Rudolph could scarcely believe what he was hearing. First, his mathematics professor had suggested he terminate his study of that subject. Then, Professor Fossbaum told him he was not good enough to study art at Oxford. Now, Fossbaum offered to accept him as a private art student, then arrange his admission to the largest art school in the nation, followed by further study in Paris. Rudolph's thoughts were interrupted by the professor, who was again standing and looking out the window. "Best go see the registrar," he said. "Get things settled. See you first Monday of the new term. And remember, the utmost diligence!" Rudolph, still in a daze, stood up, mumbled a thank you to the professor, and left the office.

It took several days for Rudolph to fully accept the reality of what had happened. It was not until Professor Fossbaum delivered the shocking news of an opportunity to study art full-time that he realized he really did want to do just that. However, elated as he was at the prospect of studying art, he was apprehensive about informing his father of the change in career. He delayed the conversation with his father until the beginning of the next term. Not only did doing so allow Rudolph time to think through how he would tell his father, but waiting until he had started his tutelage under Professor Fossbaum bolstered his own commitment to this new direction.

Although he dreaded doing so, Rudolph knew he must have a conversation with his father about giving up the study of mathematics. He expected his father would at the least be disappointed, and very possibly quite upset. He owed his entrance to Oxford at least partially to his father's influence, and his father had invested a fair sum of money in Rudolph's study there. At the worst, he imagined his father might refuse him further financial support. Since he would almost certainly receive no scholarship monies at the University of the Arts, this would crush Rudolph's hopes of studying there. But there was no avoiding the inevitable. The second weekend following the start of the new term, Rudolph took the train home to see his father.

The visit home went better than expected. On the return trip back to Oxford, Rudolph realized that he had misjudged how his father would react to his change of plans. Rather than oppose the idea or attempt to persuade his son to continue to study maths, the elder Chudzik had patiently listened to his son explain everything that occurred. He sat quietly as he heard about the mathematics professor snooping in his son's notebook and the impersonal art professor's assessment of Rudolph's abilities and proposed career path. Then in a calm, level voice, he said, "This reminds me of when I was about your age. My father wanted me to stay in Poland and become a dentist. At first, I agreed. But then things in Poland got difficult. I decided to come to England, and at the same time decided to go into business. You are also deciding to leave one place and go to another, and to leave one plan behind and begin a new one. You are doing just what I did."

His father's approval helped resolve any lingering doubts Rudolph may have felt about the decision he had made. He worked extremely hard at his new course of study, and he simultaneously endured and appreciated his private sessions with Professor Fossbaum. The professor was highly critical, sharply pointing out the smallest of flaws in his student's work and allowing only infrequent compliments on work well done. But he also occasionally showed great patience in demonstrating and helping his students learn and perfect a new technique. When the professor was particularly critical, Rudolph reminded himself that he was the beneficiary of a rare opportunity and suppressed any temptation to protest.

Despite Professor Fossbaum's critical demeanor (the more he worked under the man, the more Rudolph understood why other students called him Professor Fuss Bomb), it was clear to both teacher and student that considerable progress was being made. When he looked at his own work, Rudolph recognized that he had made rapid strides which would have been impossible except for the excellent guidance received from the art professor. He also knew that few other students worked as hard as he did to learn the intricacies of drawing and painting.

About a month prior to the end of term, during one of the private lessons, an unexpected outburst from Professor Fossbaum completely startled Rudolph and nearly made him wonder if his teacher was going mental. Rudolph was intently working on an oil painting of a country scene. The professor was looking over his shoulder when he suddenly shouted, "No, no! This will not do! Stop at once!" Rudolph turned around and looked at the professor. The man was in a state of considerable agitation. The shouting continued, "Creativity! You must have creativity!" Rudolph sat still, completely perplexed.

After a couple of moments, the professor seemed a bit less distressed. He paced up and down, muttering to himself, sometimes glancing at Rudolph's painting. Then he stopped. "No more today," he said, only slightly louder than usual. "You will stay away the rest of the week. Next week, you come with new work from which I want only two things!" Rudoph waited for more instruction. The professor continued, "First, nothing must look like anything real. Nothing! Second, use no ordinary colors. None!" Professor Fossbaum turned on his heel and left the room, leaving his student perplexed but determined to follow his teacher's instruction.

The professor's tantrum and demands to forsake real images and "ordinary" colors proved to be a turning point in Rudolph's art education. At first frustrated by his teacher's challenge, he soon embraced these new parameters. His work was admittedly unusual, but also creative and fresh. Professor Fossbaum encouraged him to stretch the limits of form and color even farther, and his paintings began to assume a distinctive style. Fellow art students expressed admiration for Rudolph's work, and he began to demonstrate heightened confidence by signing his paintings in large script, "Chudzik". Although the art professor remained critical, it was apparent that his critiques of Rudolph's paintings were more like those directed toward a colleague than toward a young student.

One week prior to the end of the term, Rudolph entered the studio for another lesson with Professor Fossbaum. On his easel he saw an envelope with his name neatly printed on it. He opened it, took out a half-sheet of paper and read, "Chudzik, no lesson today. It is not needed. Word came that your application to the University of the Arts has been accepted. Well done. Fossbaum." Then he noticed something written on the back side of the paper. He turned in over, read it, and burst out laughing. It read, "p.s. Lobbing a few fuss bombs in your direction was not such a bad idea, eh?"

The faculty at University of the Arts quickly recognized the artistic talent of Rudolph Chudzik. He worked extremely hard, progressed rapidly, and within eighteen months saw his works included in several public exhibitions. His name was known among both students and faculty, some of whom predicted it would someday be widely known among contemporary artists, likely well beyond Britain. After graduating with honors, Rudolph moved to Paris, where he studied with acquaintances of Professor Fossbaum. There, he further refined his style of non-representational painting. Within fewer than five years, the name Chudzik was frequently heard in the galleries of Paris and other cities on the continent.

By the time he reached the age of 35, Rudolph Chuznik was one of the most renowned contemporary artists in Europe. Thanks to the creativity and abstract symbolism shown in his work, his paintings were displayed in elite galleries. When auctioned, they consistently brought top prices. He continued to push the limits of form and color, and expanded his themes to include what critics termed his periode sombre (dark period). When displayed for public viewing, his periode sombre pieces always included detailed descriptions of the symbolism and ultimate meaning of each work. Rudolph declined to write them himself, and art critics and academics vied for the opportunity to compose these descriptions.

As a highly successful artist, Rudolph enjoyed an income commensurate with his popularity. His paintings, especially his periode sombre works, often sold for impressive sums. He accepted few commissions, but it was rumored that those that were accepted entailed prices in the six figures. One would be hard pressed to name any benefit of a successful art career that was not enjoyed by Rudolph Chuznik. He was at the very peak of his profession, and every serious student of contemporary art knew his name, his reputation, and his work. He had, in fact, reached the point where one might ask if there was anything more to which he could aspire.

Rudolph did ask that question, and his answer was as unique as his artwork. Numerous times over the years, he had hinted that some of his paintings were taken more seriously than was appropriate. He even went so far as to publicly question whether the prices paid at auction for some of his works were justifiable. An article in Le Monde quoted him as saying that the work produced during his periode sombre could be taken seriously or taken as a joke. This, of course, brought a flurry of responses from art critics and academics who wondered whether Rudolph Chuznik was not only a brilliant painter but also his own best PR person.

While much of the art world was paying attention to the stir over Chuznik's seemingly flippant attitude toward his own work, Rudolph decided to capitalize on this wave of attention. He returned to England, where he announced that a new exhibition of his work was to be held at The Tate Modern in London. In a headline-grabbing statement, he let the art world know that this new exhibition would include "a surprise that, when revealed, will shock even the most seasoned, the most knowledgeable, the most jaded observers and critics of contemporary art." As expected, the art world was buzzing with speculation.

Two weeks later, Rudolph Chuznik dropped another public relations bomb when he announced via the London Times an additional aspect of the mysterious surprise expected at the Tate exhibition. The second announcement confirmed the surprise promised by the initial statement but added a detail that had critics shaking their heads in bewilderment. Yes, the secret surprise would be in full view at the Tate. And it would be unique, shocking, possibly even disturbing. But the full secret itself would not be revealed until one year later, months after the exhibit closed.

This new information prompted rampant speculation on the part of critics, connoisseurs, academics, and ordinary museum patrons. What type of surprise? Why secret? If secret, how will people know when they see it? Is it going to be obscene? Has he invented a whole new style? Is it all a farce? Discussion of these and dozens of other questions filled the art columns of newspapers. Experts gave their opinions, other experts debunked the opinions of those who spoke first, and columnists tried to appear insightful without saying anything specific for which they could later be criticized. But everyone agreed on one thing, Chuznik had captured the attention of the art world like never before.

On the opening day of the Tate exhibition, people stood in queues for hours. The crowd could simply not be accommodated, and those remaining in line at closing time were told to try again the following day. This continued for nearly a week, when the capacity of the museum finally matched the number of people who came to see the Chuznik exhibition and its secret surprise. As usual, each painting was accompanied by a written commentary prepared by experts in the field of contemporary art. Viewers moved slowly through the exhibit, carefully reading each commentary, convinced the words were the key to discovering the mysterious surprise. Some people reading the commentaries claimed to have discovered clues that could reveal the secret, but others rejected their assertions.

Debate and conjecture about the secret surprise continued after the exhibit closed. The Tate Modern recorded record attendance during the exhibition and published a special brochure commemorating the event. Collectors were anticipating unusually high prices if the exhibited works were released for sale, and pressed auction houses for information about likely bidding opportunities. Media organizations interviewed Rudolph Chuznik, hoping he might purposely or inadvertently reveal the nature of the surprise, giving them a scoop that could boost their popularity. But despite all the commotion, people were forced to wait until the one-year anniversary of the exhibition opening.

Rudolph had decided to reveal the surprise at the Tate in a special gathering hosted by the museum's managing director. The top names in the world of contemporary art were in attendance. Artists, critics, collectors, gallery owners, heads of auction houses, museum curators, academics, and media personalities from across Europe listened to introductory remarks from the head of the Tate, followed by talks by several leading critics. Noone had seen Rudolph Chuznik in the throng, and people assumed he was sequestered in a room somewhere until his turn to speak. Finally, it was time for the main item on the agenda, the reveal of the secret surprise. As the managing director of the museum read the introduction, a screen descended from the ceiling behind the podium. The museum head finished the introduction and sat down.

The lights were dimmed, and an image of Rudolph Chuznik appeared on the screen. The crowd gasped as they realized he was not in the room, but only on video. The image on the screen smiled and began to speak. "Thank you all for coming," Rudolph said. "You may wonder why I am not there with you as I reveal the surprise as I promised a year ago. Frankly, I am not certain how you will react to the truth about the exhibition. So please forgive my absence." Some of the audience looked disappointed, but everyone remained attentive to the screen. Rudolph continued, "As with all exhibits of my work, each piece displayed there at the Tate had posted next to it an expert analysis of the work. These commentaries were written by noted critics and academics, most of which are there with you tonight."

Some of the commentaries' authors sat more upright, making it easier for others to recognize them. Rudolph continued, "It is no secret that I have suggested from time to time that we all may take our work a bit too seriously. In fact, as you know, despite my appreciation for the lifestyle I have enjoyed, thanks to those who do take my work seriously, I have questioned whether many of my works – and by implication many others' works as well – should command the prices that they do. Of course, many of you would argue that they are worth the prices paid. You justify the price based less on a work's visual appeal and more on the message, the symbolism, the deep meaning expressed by an image that to the unschooled seems to represent nothing at all." Some of the guests shifted in their seats, most were not smiling.

Rudolph resumed speaking. "Now I want to tell you about the secret I promised to reveal tonight. I'm going to let this distinguished group of experts be the first to know what it was that escaped discovery by so many museum visitors over so many weeks. Not only that, but it was not uncovered by any of you present this evening. Not by any of my fellow artists, or critics, or academics, or anyone else who understands the world of art, including those who were given the responsibility of writing the descriptions of each work displayed during the exhibit. These commentaries were read by many thousands of people, and no doubt by everyone in attendance tonight. Which brings me to the surprise. For the entire length of the exhibit, each and every one of those carefully constructed, expertly insightful commentaries on the paintings shown were purposely posted next to paintings different from the ones for which they were written. That is the truth. I'll leave it to you to explain to the public tomorrow. Good night."

The lights came up. Eyes darted around the room, which was filled with the sound of murmuring, hushed conversation. One man began to laugh, but quickly grew silent. Some sat still in quiet disbelief. A few people stood up and headed for the exit. The head of a leading museum was heard to say, "He really did, didn't he?" and his companion replied, "Wouldn't have thought it, myself." Then they joined those walking toward the exit.

2

THE BANKER

A tall man dressed in tan slacks, a pale-yellow shirt with an open collar, and a brown tweed sportcoat entered the bank. He nodded to a middle-aged man standing next to the nearest teller window, who returned the nod. Neither man spoke. The tall man did not join the customers waiting at the row of teller windows but walked directly toward a door marked "Employees Only". He opened the door, walked into the room behind it, and heard a woman's voice say, "Good afternoon, Mr. Wilson." Without slowing his walk or turning his head toward the voice, he forced a half-smile and said, "Good for you, I hope, Nancy." There were two offices adjacent to the anteroom that held the desk of his assistant, Nancy Collins. He entered the larger of the two offices, removed his sportscoat and hung it on a dark wooden rack in the corner, and sat down in a large leather chair behind his desk.

Miss Collins gave a perfunctory rap on his office door and walked in. "So," she said, "is our favorite bank president having not the best day?" She sounded genuinely sympathetic, despite the frequency with which Lloyd Wilson seemed determined to garner sympathy by complaining. He shook his head. "Not just a bad day," he replied, "but a bad week. TGIF is all I've got to say." Nancy Collins raised her eyebrows and shrugged her shoulders. "Well, it's like this every time the bank examiners are here. I know they're a pain, but they're almost done." "It's about time!" the banker replied. "Not only have they been here more days than they told me they would be, but the way they "request" files and so on ... you'd think I was a junior teller, not the president of the bank." During their conversation, Lloyd had opened a large envelope his assistant had placed on his desk. He scanned the contents, frowned, and placed it in the trash.

Nancy Collins, accustomed to her boss's mannerisms, waited until he looked up at her. "Well," she said, "like you say, TGIF. And there are only a couple of hours of "F" left. Next week will be better." "I hope so," the banker replied, "There's only one way to go from here, and that's up." His assistant turned to leave the office, then remembered something. "Your wife wants you to call her," she said, "something about tomorrow's event, I think." "Get her for me, will you?" Mr. Wilson commanded. Miss Collins left her boss's office, and a short time later his phone buzzed. The banker picked it up and was connected to his spouse.

Mrs. Wilson spoke first. "How's your day going, dear?" she asked. "Oh, it could be worse," he replied, "those darn examiners are still here. Such pests. But they should be done today. How about yours?" "Oh, busy as you might expect," she said. "Everyone on the committee is trying to make sure Agnes Clayton Day comes off just right. Which reminds me, Lloyd, did you pick up the programs from the printer and the award for Agnes from the trophy shop?" "I got the programs, just got back a little while ago," he said, "and I'll get the plaque on my way home. Unless the darn examiners decide to lock me in the bank all night." "They couldn't do that, could they?" Mrs. Wilson asked. "No, no, Karen," he replied, "I was kidding. I'll get out of here at the usual time. See you later." As he hung up the phone, he heard his wife say something, and thought of calling her back. But he had things to finish before the examiner meeting, and he was determined to get that over with as soon as possible.

Despite his grumbling and outward pessimism, Lloyd Wilson was actually quite satisfied with his circumstances and proud of his accomplishments. After college and a short stint in a large bank in the state capital, he accepted a mid-level position at a bank in a downstate community of about four thousand people. He worked hard, earned an opportunity to buy into the bank, and after a dozen years became the president. Like all people, Lloyd Wilson had strong points and shortcomings. Some people disliked his constant complaining, but most dismissed that trait with a casual "that's just Lloyd."

He was careful who he hired, treated the bank's staff well, and had very little turnover. The head teller had been with the bank nearly twenty years, and the other tellers averaged nearly fifteen. When he first assumed control of the bank, Lloyd had made the unconventional move of promoting a female to the position of vice-president and head of the loan department. She quickly proved herself one of the most dedicated members of his staff. In fact, her commitment to the bank was exemplary. She had no prior connection to the area, and reportedly relocated after a nasty divorce. Hired by the bank, she developed a reputation as a hard worker and a supporter of a variety of activities beneficial to the community. She made her job the center of her life and built strong relationships with customers by personally managing a large share of the bank's loan accounts. She was, as Lloyd Wilson once said, "The person you would get if you rubbed a genie's lamp and wished for the best employee ever."

Lloyd Wilson was ready for his meeting with the bank examiners, which was scheduled for four o'clock. They were late, and as he waited, he found himself comparing them to his female vice-president. "If they had one-tenth of her ambition and dedication," he said to himself, "they would have been out of here two days ago at the latest." Hopefully, the meeting would be little more than a formality; a brief overview of the results, and a few minor suggestions for improvement. He glanced at the clock. "Fifteen minutes late," he thought, "inexcusable."

Just then, his phone rang. He waited for his assistant to answer it, then remembered he had given her permission to leave early. He picked it up and heard a familiar voice. "Lloyd, I just got a call from the trophy shop. They said they're finishing up the plaque and want to make sure the inscription is right. Can I read what they have?" "Sure, Karen," he said, with a hint of exasperation, "let's hope they can get something this simple right the first time." His wife said, "Three lines. First line, congratulations. Second line, Agnes Clayton Day. Third line, tomorrow's date. Is that OK?" "I feel like I'm playing charades," Lloyd responded. "It's fine. Gotta go. The examiners are finally done." He hung up the phone, glanced at the clock again, and resumed thinking about his favorite employee.

"Agnes Clayton," he thought. "This bank is lucky to have a person with her qualities. Smart, hardworking, conservative, and completely dedicated. Plus, not too good-looking, and after a bitter divorce, likely to remain single and employed." He smiled to himself. Then, he got out of his chair, walked out of his office, and opened the door to the office next to it.

A man and a woman were sitting at a table in the office, engaged in intense, hushed conversation. Piles of paper were spread on the table amid a laptop computer and printer. Between the two people was a mobile phone, evidently on speaker. The woman, leaning toward the phone, said, "Bill, we're going to have to finish this conversation later. We need to meet with the bank president now. We'll email our summary this evening from the motel." The man turned to Lloyd. "Mr. Wilson," he said, "I apologize for taking so long. But rest assured, we have done a thorough examination of your bank's activities. And we're ready to discuss the results." Lloyd nodded and suggested they move to his office, since it was larger and more comfortable.

Lloyd returned to his office and sat behind his desk. He motioned for the man and woman to take seats directly in front of him. He noticed they both seemed very serious, which he thought was probably standard for their occupation, but decided a bit of levity might be a good way to begin the conversation. "OK," he said, "I've got to get home and help my wife get ready for a big event in town tomorrow, so if I'm going to jail tell me right up front." He chuckled at his remark. Neither the man nor the woman smiled. The man said. "As you know, we talked with several of your employees. They were helpful." The woman added, "None of them were anything other than cooperative." Lloyd was getting irritated. "Why are they beating around the bush?" he wondered. "Didn't they get my hint about hurrying so I can get home to help Karen get ready for tomorrow?"

The man spoke again. "You have some interesting employees," he said. "Your head teller ... how long has he been here?" "I'd have to look, but eighteen, maybe nineteen years," Lloyd said. "Something unusual about that?" "No, not especially," the man replied, turning to the woman. Lloyd looked at the female member of the examining team. She seemed nervous and looked like she was under some type of strain. The woman pulled her chair a bit closer to Lloyd's desk and said, "Tell us about your VP of the loan department."

Lloyd smiled. "Ah, Agnes," he said, "No wonder you noticed her. She is absolutely the most loyal and dedicated person I have ever worked with. Agnes Clayton has done more for this bank than anybody besides myself." "I see," the woman said. "Anything else significant about her?" "Let me just say this," Lloyd said, "Her life revolves around two things. The bank and this town. She works extremely hard and more than earns her salary, which by the way is not small. And she sets an example for our loan customers by living frugally. Her thriftiness, plus her financial acumen, have allowed her to contribute generously to many worthy causes in the community."

Lloyd wasn't sure why the woman was interested in his star employee. Perhaps she would learn something she could pass on to other bank managers. He continued, "Since you are staying in town tonight, let me invite you to attend the Citizens' Award Day tomorrow. Once a year the Chamber of Commerce honors a member of our community. It's always someone who is highly thought of and has done a lot to help the town. I was the recipient three years ago. And tomorrow ... well, tomorrow is Agnes Clayton Day. The whole town will turn out to honor her and everything she has done for this community."

Lloyd noticed that neither person sitting in front of him shared his enthusiasm for tomorrow's event. Then the man asked, "Agnes Clayton. You said she is dedicated to her job. Does she take much time off?" Lloyd thought it was an odd question, but his prior experience with bank examiners had taught him that they sometimes asked different questions than he expected. "No," Lloyd said, "she doesn't. In fact, I'd say Agnes is like we used to say about the mailman ... neither rain, nor snow, nor hail, nor whatever ... if the bank is open, she is here." The man and the woman exchanged glances. They seemed disappointed.

"Mr. Wilson," the man said, "we appreciate your invitation to attend tomorrow's ceremony, but we will have to decline. As soon as we are done here, we will print a copy of our full report for you. When you read it you will understand why. Unfortunately, I sincerely doubt you will want to attend either. It's all in our report, but it seems the generous contributions Agnes Clayton has been making for the benefit of your community did not come from her conservative habits. The money came from your bank. Agnes Clayton has, as best we can tell, been diverting loan payments from this bank to an offshore account for several years."

Lloyd Wilson sat silently staring at the man. After what seemed like several minutes, the woman spoke. "Mr. Wilson, we're going to print a copy of our full report for you now. I know this is a shock, and we're sorry it happened. But I'm going to suggest you contact law enforcement immediately. We don't want this woman to leave town as suddenly as she came." The man and woman stood and walked out of Lloyd's office.

Lloyd sat silently for several minutes, thinking about what he had just heard from the bank examiners. Then he picked up the phone and dialed. A voice answered, "Wilson's, this is Karen." Lloyd took a deep breath and said, "This is me. I want you to come down to the bank right away. We have to talk about tomorrow." "Tomorrow?" she said. "What about tomorrow? And why do I need to come down there?" "I'll explain when you get here," he said, "I've got something else to do right now." He hung up the phone, looked up another number, and dialed again. A woman's voice said, "Sheriff's Department. How may I help you?" "This is Lloyd Wilson," he said. "Tell the sheriff I need to see him at the bank right away. It's not a robbery or anything, but it's important. Tell him to come in the side door and right to my office." He hung up the phone, pushed his chair back from his desk, and sat in silence for a couple of minutes. Then, though alone in his office, he said aloud, "Agnes Clayton. I always thought there was something a little strange about her."

3

THE BARON

A note to the reader: As the main character in this story is a British royal, it may be helpful to clarify terminology related to his title. He is a baron, the lowest level of the aristocracy, which also makes him a lord. His name is Richard Addison and his title the Baron Westfield, so his full proper identity is Lord Richard Addison, the Baron Westfield. If he marries, his wife will become the Baroness Westfield, which also makes her a lady.

If one asked the residents of Chippenham and the surrounding countryside about Lord Richard Addison, the Baron Westfield, and his wife, the lovely Lady Sylvia Addison, they would likely suggest, with an attitude of deference, that the couple lived the secure and comfortable life expected of people of their status. They were, of course, looked up to by the lower classes, but were not the object of excessive envy or jealousy. The Baron and Baroness enjoyed luxury and privilege not afforded their neighbors, but that disparity was long-standing and entirely accepted.

The Baron and Baroness lived in a sizeable manor house on the estate Lord Addison had inherited from his father, the sixth Baron Westfield and the fourth owner of the estate. Lord Addison's great-great-grandfather had acquired the estate in the late 1600s as a reward from King James II for his support during the English Civil War. At various times since, portions of the estate had been sold off, eventually reaching a size of slightly less than seven hundred acres. Though not of the scale it had once been, the estate provided certain foodstuffs required by the manor house and supported a herd of finely bred sheep as well as flocks of fowl, a small number of milk cows, and a stable of some reputation. Lord Addison was proud of his horses and took a personal interest in their breeding and training. And though not as frequently as in his earlier years, he enjoyed riding to hounds with peers from the region.

Neither Lord Richard Addison nor Lady Sylvia Addison appeared to have cause for complaint about their lives. Yet the Baron's daily existence was not one of contentment and satisfaction. In fact, it was quite the opposite. Lord Addison's days were peppered with incidents that gave rise to frustration and near despair. Seldom did a day pass without multiple reminders of his unhappy state. The cause of his discontent was a single, vexing problem. It was his wife, Lady Sylvia.

When Lord Richard was a young man, he had set for himself three goals, which if attained, were to ensure his happiness and self-measured success. The first was to always remain in his father's favor, so that he would with certainty obtain his rightful inheritance and become the lord of the manor. This he accomplished through diligent obedience to his father and plying the affection of his doting mother. The second was to learn enough about business, law, and finance to capably manage and prevent further reduction in the size of the estate, thus ensuring sufficient income to live out his years comfortably and well-served in the manor house. This he did through a combination of careful attention to his father's business dealings and by leaving home long enough to earn a law degree at Cambridge. The third objective sought by young Lord Richard

Addison was to marry a truly beautiful woman whose appearance would announce to all who saw her that he was, indeed, a man who deserved and possessed the things of which other men could only dream.

While in his twenties Lord Richard had numerous potential opportunities to wed. He was titled, educated, financially stable, socially adept, and not offensive in appearance. What he may have lacked in handsomeness he made up for in an outgoing manner and practiced charm. Although he was often brusque and bordered on rudeness in his business dealing, he could, in the presence of the opposite sex, exhibit a degree of sensitivity and warmth not otherwise evident. However, despite these qualities and his mother's frequent and sincere attempts at matchmaking, Lord Richard reached his thirtieth birthday unmarried.

It was at a Christmas ball the following winter that Lord Richard Addison finally espied a woman whose appearance met his standards. All the notable families from the area surrounding Chippenham attended the annual ball, and it was not uncommon for romantic relationships to trace their origin to this holiday event. The ball began with a Grand March accompanied by a small orchestra placed at the far end of the main hall. Precisely spaced couples promenaded down the center of the hall, then separated with men forming a line on one side of the hall and women on the other. Lord Richard observed the procession from among the ranks of the younger gentlemen in attendance, silently critiquing each of the females on parade. As the fifth couple in the Grand March approached Lord Richard's position he was struck by the beauty of the young woman in front of him.

The woman, who chanced a slightly coquettish smile in his direction as she passed by, was extraordinarily attractive. She was petite, with a tiny waist, slender arms and neck, and delicate fingers. Her complexion, almost milky white except for a light blush of rose in her cheeks, was flawless. Her eyes, which brightened with her winsome smile, were of an azure hue that resembled that of a cloudless sky. Her hair, which fell in long, curling locks onto her shoulders, reminded Lord Richard of his mother's lovely auburn tresses. There was nothing in any way objectionable about the appearance of the woman, who appeared to be no more than twenty years of age.

Lord Richard, quickly recovering from the shock of having seen such a vision, immediately began to formulate a plan to gain an introduction to the young woman. He turned away from the marchers and made his way toward the edge of the gathering, from which he began to circle the crowd in search of his mother. He found her on the far side of the hall together with a lady friend, paying scant attention to the Grand March while carefully choosing selections from a table of hors d'oeuvres. A brief conversation between Lord Richard and his mother resulted in her excusing herself while handing her plate of food to her nonplussed friend, and with her son in tow, setting out to locate the young woman he had described to her.

Happily, the young woman was both easily found and instantly recognized by Lord Richard's mother. Not only did she know the identity of the young woman, but she assured Lord Richard that an introduction could be readily facilitated by one of the woman's aunts, also in attendance, and an intimate acquaintance of Lord Richard's mother. Allowing no delay, his mother immediately searched for and found the young woman's aunt, and an introduction between Lord Richard and the lovely Sylvia Strathmore occurred within minutes after the conclusion of the Grand March. Lord Richard presented a forthright request to Miss Strathmore for a dance and was gratified that she not only accepted, but seemed pleased to be asked. Two more dances together transpired during the ball, and before the evening ended Lord Richard had received the young woman's permission to call on her. His mood as he left the ball was closer to one of happiness and optimism than he had experienced in many months.

Within a week, Lord Richard made his first call at the Strathmore home, during which he again marveled at Miss Silvia's splendid appearance and gathered pertinent information about the young woman and her family. The Strathmores, though not wealthy, were known primarily for their good character and the beauty of their daughters. Sylvia Strathmore and her parents welcomed Lord Richard's visits, which occurred regularly on Sunday afternoons, and as expected resulted in Miss Silvia's accepting the Baron's proposal to marry. The couple's wedding occurred barely three months after their engagement, which townspeople attributed to encouragement from Lord Richard's mother, whose desire to secure a marriage for her son was common knowledge. The marriage ceremony, reception, and ball were a much-discussed highlight of the Chippenham social season, which immensely pleased the Baron's mother. The bride and groom toured for four weeks on the continent, returning to the family's estate in time for the start of the hunting season.

The new couple began their lives together on a happy note. Lord Richard Addison basked in the delight of having married a beautiful woman some twelve years his junior, while the former Miss Strathmore accustomed herself to her new status as Lady Addison, the Baroness Westfield. Lord Richard was kept busy overseeing the estate's grounds and the manor house staff, to the extent that he found it necessary to decline several hunting invitations. Lady Addison was content to let her husband manage the household and spent her time either socializing or attending to the myriad items essential to maintaining her physical attractiveness. Given access to Lord Richard's funds, she was not hesitant to order the latest fashions and highest quality cosmetics from London suppliers. She fastidiously attended to her diet, facials, massages, milk baths, and the other things required to retain the beauty which had won her entry to the world of peerage.

Lord Richard encouraged his wife to become active in managing the household, but she refused on the grounds that dealing with staff induced stress that affected body chemistry and harmed one's complexion. Lady Sylvia also declined Lord Richard's repeated invitations to join in hiking, riding, fishing, hunting, and other outdoor activities on the estate due to the negative effects wind and sun had on her fair skin. The Baron was irritated by his wife's rejection of activities and responsibilities in which he had assumed she would engage, but also realized her priorities allowed him to continue the pursuits he had enjoyed as a single man.

Lady Sylvia did, however, willingly accompany her husband on carriage rides into Chippenham, where she invariably drew the attention of the citizenry. Her reputation for beauty was thoroughly known, and when Lord and Lady Addison's carriage entered the village, the younger men would actually vie with each other for a position on the side of the road which placed them nearest Lady Sylvia as she passed by. Invariably, when the couple alit from the carriage to enter a shop or to call on friends, nearby men and women looked intently at the couple, and often within hearing range, remarked about Lady Sylvia's beautiful appearance. She did wonder how her husband perceived this phenomenon, but need not have concerned herself, as Lord Richard took great pleasure in the obvious envy of other men.

Lord Richard's courtship of his carefully selected spouse had been rather brief, and in accord with the custom of the time, had permitted very little time for the couple to be alone. Their visits were chaperoned, and their verbal exchanges did not address weighty subjects or include topics that might reveal the levels of knowledge or conversation skills of either party. As was common, the couple married without either knowing well the other's personal attributes, interests, or mannerisms. Lord Richard knew his bride was exceptionally beautiful, and Miss Sylvia knew her groom was titled, wealthy, and politely charming. Thus, the couple began their marriage with the assurance that each had managed to gain a spouse that met their respective requirements.

During the early months of their marriage the lives of Lord Richard and the newly titled Lady Sylvia Addison progressed uneventfully, and the couple settled into a routine in which they spent most of their waking hours apart from one another. Lord Richard arose early and enjoyed a full breakfast. He then summoned the estate's farm manager, had a horse saddled, and rode with his manager to inspect the grounds and fields. Lady Sylvia arose late, tended to her personal grooming, and joined her husband for a light meal after he returned from his ride. After their midday meal together, Lord Richard read the day's London Times, then either tended to his correspondence and did some reading in the library, or when the opportunity arose, joined some of his peers for a hunt. Lady Sylvia generally took a beauty nap, then either dressed and prepared herself for receiving or calling on one or more of her lady friends, or spent the afternoon reading her favorite works of fiction. On their at-home evenings, the couple dined together, then spent the evening reading or engaging in hobbies or games that involved minimal conversation. Beyond the necessary, they talked little, which seemed to suit them both. Lady Sylvia neither understood nor showed much interest in the affairs of the estate, and Lord Richard was equally disinterested in the social news his wife acquired during her visits with her friends.

Lord and Lady Addison's relationship was workable and appeared to be stable enough during the first few years of their marriage. The difference in their ages did not seem to be problematic, especially since both had agreed they did not want to have children, and careful management of the estate had increased its assets and expanded the Baron's land holdings. The couple kept a busy social calendar, and Lady Sylvia was, as always, a focus of admiration at the many dinners, balls, and parties the couple attended. Lord Richard enjoyed attending to the details of the estate, and although he wished Lady Sylvia had assumed an active role in managing the household staff, he coped with that responsibility with little complaint. He always looked forward to the various hunting seasons, the experiences of which proved useful as topics of conversation among the men at the numerous social gatherings he was obligated to attend. And he was pleased that his finances were in good order. Those who knew the couple were certain that all was well with Lord and Lady Addison.

Yet, within a half dozen years of his marriage to Sylvia Strathmore, all was not well with Lord Richard Addison. Despite his continued admiration for his wife's physical beauty, he became conscious of a noticeable and recurring negative feeling toward his spouse. In analyzing the situation, he first thought the cause of his discontent might be Lady Sylvia's extreme attention to her appearance. She treated, primped, and preened herself daily, and invested hours preparing herself for social events. But he was seldom present while she tended to her rituals of baths, creams, and cosmetics, and had to acknowledge that he greatly admired the result of her efforts. He then considered the possibility that the monies spent with London fashion purveyors might be disturbing his emotional equilibrium. But he rejected this idea because he knew he had paid scant attention to the actual amounts involved, and rather than expressing displeasure had in fact frequently complimented Lady Sylvia on the stylishness of her purchases. It was only when he consciously recalled specific instances when his feelings of dissatisfaction were most pronounced that he was able to pinpoint their cause.

Lord Richard realized there were two types of situations in which he actually felt disturbed by his wife's behavior, situations which he realized were both ordinary and frequent. In fact, so ordinary and occurring so often that he wondered how he could have remained largely unaware for so many months. The first type of circumstance was the numerous instances where Lord Richard and Lady Sylvia were together with other couples, discussing topics of no more depth than those usually included in casual conversations among friends. It struck Lord Richard that he was often embarrassed by his wife's lack of understanding about the most ordinary subjects. Even when the conversation turned to such mundane topics as the weather, recent balls or parties, or even local gossip, Lady Sylvia would invariably either have nothing to contribute or make comments so inane or unrelated to the topic at hand that the others present would look at Lord Richard with an unmistakable questioning expression.

The other situation in which Lord Richard's feelings toward his wife turned negative was when he and his wife spent their evening together at the manor house. During these times, the couple did not have unpleasant or disagreeable conversations. Rather, they hardly conversed at all. Early in their marriage, he had tried to make conversation regarding various aspects of the estate's activities, household management, or other business dealings. Over time, Lord Richard concluded that his wife not only had no interest in such topics, but evidently also lacked the ability to comprehend them. Lady Sylvia, meanwhile, found that her husband was patently uninterested in her primary concerns, which included her social life, the planning of parties and balls, and the news, rumors, and gossip regarding the Chippenham residents and others in the couple's social circle. Thus, both husband and wife turned increasingly to their own interests, and seldom engaged in what could be described as meaningful conversation.

There are undoubtedly men who, finding themselves in a relationship similar to that of Lord Richard Addison, would recognize that their choice of spouse had not been optimal but was largely of their own doing, and could be well endured for as long as necessary, potentially a lifetime. But Lord Richard was not one of them. What began as an occasional irritation over his wife's lack of interest and intelligence grew into a frequent frustration, and then an intense dissatisfaction that increasingly occupied his mind. Over a period of months, the intense admiration he had always felt for his wife's beauty began to fade, replaced by a severe dislike for her shortcomings.

Lord Richard was a man who, having thought through a situation, decided upon a solution and was at once committed to enacting a plan to achieve his objective. Having applied his usual logic to the increasingly unsatisfactory marriage, he concluded that his wife's beauty had been overvalued and had obscured serious deficiencies that resulted in his unhappy circumstance. Because she showed neither the inclination nor the capacity to improve her intellectual status, the most practical solution to this dilemma was to divorce Lady Sylvia. He could then either return to the relatively pleasant life as the unmarried Baron Westfield, or perhaps at an appropriate point select a wife who possessed a better balance of beauty and intellect. The challenge would be to structure the divorce in a manner which would retain his reputation and social standing,

ideally by removing Lady Sylvia from the community and settling upon her a stipend of a reasonable amount. Too paltry
an amount would encourage others to view the Baron as cal-
lous, whereas too large a sum might lead others to think him
reckless or extravagant. All these things he thought through
carefully, then devised a plan.

Although Lord Richard held a law degree, he knew that
successful implementation of his plan required the services of
a solicitor specializing in marriage law. A few discreet inquiries led him to a highly respected law firm in London, which
he visited during what he described to his wife as an urgent
estate matter. The desired provisions of the divorce were discussed and noted, and Lord Richard was promised completion
of all related legal documents within a fortnight. He had gone
to London bearing the burden of a weighty problem, but on
the return train to Chippenham he felt his troubles had been
halved. He would wait one week, then tell Lady Sylvia that a
second trip to London was required. He would invite her to
accompany him and suggest that she use her time in London
to visit some of the establishments from which she sourced
her clothing and beauty supplies. Once in London, he would
convince her to join him for just a brief business discussion,
after which she could resume her shopping. That meeting
would take place at the solicitor's office, where the divorce
documents would be waiting. If all went according to plan, and
it was a careful plan, she would acquiesce to leaving the Chippenham area in return for an increase in the proposed stipend.
She would return briefly to the estate, pack and arrange shipping of her clothing and other possessions to whatever place
she chose to relocate, and his objective would be met.

Two weeks later, Lord and Lady Addison prepared to board
the train in Chippenham, bound for Charing Cross Station,
London. Lady Sylvia Addison, arrayed in her usual finery,

attracted the attention of the other waiting passengers, and it was obvious that they were admiring her. Although it perhaps should not have, this took Lord Richard somewhat by surprise, as he had for several months been so focused on the issues in their relationship that he had virtually ignored her appearance and the attention it brought. He overheard several comments about his wife's beauty and sense of fashion. One woman went so far as to ask her companion why a woman as lovely as Lady Sylvia would marry an obviously older man. He was at first offended by her remark, but then realized it was in a sense a compliment to both him and his wife. He pondered this while he waited for the train.

Once aboard, Lord and Lady Addison shared a compartment with an obviously affluent couple who had boarded at a previous station. When Lord Richard and Lady Sylvia entered the compartment, the man and woman both stared at them to an impolite degree. The strangers, realizing what they had done, attempted to recover their aplomb by saying they were surprised to be expected to share the compartment, which both couples knew was false. During the ensuing introductions, the man, who could not seem to divert his eyes from Lady Sylvia, felt his face flush and heard himself stammer like a schoolboy. The poor fellow was totally overwhelmed by the loveliness of the woman before him. Lord Richard was not sure what to make of this display, so simply introduced himself, shook hands, and took his seat. As the train got underway, he replayed in his mind the awkward introductions and the man's reaction to seeing Lady Sylvia for the first time.

After about an hour's travel, Lady Sylvia suggested to Lord Richard that they go to the dining car for tea. She led the way and as he followed, he noticed the expressions on the faces of the people they passed. Like the couple in their compartment, the other passengers were obviously noticing his wife, and like those waiting at the station in Chippenham, audibly commenting on her strikingly beautiful appearance. He thought they must be wondering why such a gorgeous woman was with a man of his age and appearance. He imagined them thinking that he might be her older brother, or perhaps her uncle or guardian. When they reached the dining car, he asked for a table at the far end of the car. The fewer people walked past their table, the fewer looks and comments they would be subjected to. Lord Richard did not anticipate the actions of the waiter, who returned to their table twice to affirm the correctness of their order, transparently for the purpose of gazing at the beautiful Lady Sylvia.

It had been some time since Lord Richard had seriously thought about his wife's attractiveness and the rarity of her physical perfection. It seemed that every interaction on the train, at Charing Cross Station, at their hotel, at the restaurant where they ate that evening, was another opportunity for strangers to remind Lord Richard that the woman with him was incredibly beautiful and they didn't understand why she was with him. Through their eyes and his imaginings of their thoughts, he began to see his companion as he had when he first met the lovely Miss Sylvia Strathmore, and when he courted Miss Sylvia, and when she became Lady Sylvia Addison, the Baroness Westfield. As they returned to the hotel for the night, he seemed in a state of mental confusion. He watched her bedtime ritual, the multiple steps she took to preserve her beauty, and was amazed. Then he recalled the purpose of their trip, and he was struck by the incongruity of her beauty and the shallowness of their relationship. It was with these thoughts in his mind that he drifted off to sleep.

The next morning at breakfast Lady Sylvia, who had agreed to accompany her husband to a business meeting and was not looking forward to the event, asked him how far it was to the office where the meeting would be held, and how long the meeting would last. To her surprise, rather than answering her questions, he excused himself and stepped out of the dining room and walked directly to the concierge desk. She watched as he gave some sort of instructions to the man behind the desk. He then wrote something on a piece of paper, appeared to sign it, put it in an envelope and handed it to the concierge. The two men spoke just a bit more, then shook hands, and Lord Richard returned to his wife. She had no idea what had just taken place, but simply smiled and repeated her earlier questions.

Lord Richard's reply was not expected by his wife. He told her there had been a change in plans. The business meeting was cancelled, and they would be taking the late afternoon train back to Chippenham. In the time available prior to the transport he had arranged to Charing Cross Station, she may as well continue her shopping. And he would gladly accompany her, as he might learn something about women's fashion. Lady Sylvia, caught totally by surprise, had even less to say than usual. She smiled at her husband, her eyes sparkling, and held out her hand. He took it and squeezed it gently. Just then, the waiter approached and placed the cheque on their table. With obvious embarrassment, he said he hoped that Lady Sylvia would not be offended, but he wanted to tell her she was the most beautiful woman he had ever seen.

Lord Richard, who had never been known to fraternize with the waitstaff, stood facing the man and shook his hand. He smiled at the waiter and told him that he had never heard a man make a truer statement. He then turned, gesturing to his wife to lead the way toward the dining room exit. He followed her across the room, knowing he would find delight in the expressions and comments of the strangers they passed.

4

THE BENEFACTOR

Despite its name, Newtown was in reality more an English village than a town. During the time coal mining and iron smelting flourished in the area it had been a prosperous community with a population exceeding seven thousand souls. The rail line which passed through Newtown had seen a good deal of traffic as coal and iron were transported to the industrial centers further south and as people on day trips or on holiday arrived by train to visit the area. The tourists came for just one reason: to see a single building that was the sole attraction to those from outside the local area. They came to see Saint Anthony's Church.

The original Saint Anthony's, built in the early 1700s, was a structure typical for the time and circumstance. It served the needs of Newtown until 1871, when it was destroyed by fire. A replacement was needed. Fortuitously, planning for the new building coincided with both a boom in the coal market and increased demand for iron as builders transitioned from wrought iron to steel. As a result, the wealth of many citizens of Newtown escalated rapidly. The community, largely populated by faithful church attendees, reached a consensus that the new Saint Anthony's must reflect the area's burgeoning prosperity and the townspeople's Christian devotion. Thus the people of Newtown committed to create a structure that far exceeded the practical needs of the community and would, as recorded in the town meeting records, "visually represent the glory of God on earth."

An architectural firm from London was hired with directions to design an edifice that would "rival or exceed any church building currently existing in any town or city with a population up to ten times that of Newtown." This challenge exempted from comparison only about twenty cities in all of England. When the architect who was assigned the project tried to persuade the Newtown officials that their requirements were unwarranted and over time might prove to be financially unsustainable, the officials promptly requested a different architect. The replacement architect proved much more amenable to the town's wishes.

The design of the new Saint Anthony's spared no expense, with Italian marble, German wood carvings, and stained-glass windows from France. The focal points of the interior were an ornate altar, above which hung a twenty-foot painting of the crucifixion, and, behind the rear balcony, a pipe organ magnificent in both sound and appearance. By assembling a work crew more than twice the usual size, the builders completed construction in just nine years.

The result was remarkable. Never had any mid-sized town in England dreamed of possessing such an amazing and beautiful structure, let alone raised the funds required to realize such a dream. Set on a hill in the center of Newtown, the new Saint Anthony's appeared from a distance more like a glistening castle than a parish church. All who came to see it were overwhelmed by the structure's grandeur and incredible beauty. Lord Arthur, a nobleman who visited shortly after the building's dedication, described Saint Anthony's as "simply astonishing, heavenly, and worthy of both praise and support." Apparently he was serious in his reference to support, as he soon thereafter pledged one thousand pounds per year toward the building's upkeep.

As the reputation of the new Saint Anthony's spread, Newtown became a highly desirable destination for travelers throughout England and beyond. Hundreds of people per day descended on the community, prompting expansion of rail schedules and stimulating growth in the number of inns and public houses. Travel companies began to sponsor trips that included one or two nights in Newtown, even though Saint Anthony's Church was virtually the only thing of interest to tourists. The future of Newtown seemed secure, and the town's leaders congratulated themselves on the success of what a few citizens had warned was an unreasonable plan and outlandish expenditure. The crowds of strangers continually arriving in Newtown to view the amazing new church building attested to the correctness of the town's extraordinary undertaking.

The prosperity of Newtown continued unabated for more than a decade. Then, the national economy went through an adjustment and demand for coal declined. Soon thereafter, other sources of iron became available at lower cost, and the area surrounding Newtown felt the effects of these changes. Jobs were lost, property was ceded, and the population of the town shrunk. The tourist trade remained strong, but Newtown declined rapidly. Within a decade the town's population was half what it had been during construction of Saint Anthony's, and the shrinkage continued. Soon the remaining parishioners of Saint Anthony's found themselves unable to fund the required maintenance and upkeep of their magnificent church. In fact, the church was behind budget and in debt more than eight thousand pounds. The future had turned from brightly optimistic to bleakly worrisome.

It was during the summer of 1895 that the rector of Saint Anthony's received a letter from a London-based solicitor. The letter stated that the man would arrive in Newtown on the next afternoon's train and that he would explain to the rector his purpose when the two men met. The rector was surprised to learn that the solicitor had grown up in a village near Newtown and had for a time sung in the Saint Anthony's boys choir. The solicitor arrived as planned and informed the rector that he represented a client who wished to make an anonymous gift to the parish in the amount of ten thousand pounds. Furthermore, the anonymous donor intended to repeat this generous act on an annual basis. The benefactor only required that the rector communicate quarterly to the solicitor the financial state of the church.

The reaction of the townspeople was predictable. There was a combination of relief, sincere gratitude, and palpable curiosity regarding the anonymous donor. The solicitor, bound by promise to his client, revealed not so much as a single hint as to the identity of the person who sent the gift to Saint Anthony's. The citizens of Newtown accepted both the gift and the condition of anonymity and applied the bulk of the gift toward upkeep of the church building that had been delayed due to lack of funds.

In the ensuing years the rector fulfilled the solicitor's request for periodic financial information, and each summer another sizeable gift arrived from the unknown benefactor. The amount of the gift varied from year to year but was always sufficient to ensure the beauty of Saint Anthony's was fully preserved. The parishioners, to their credit, continued to give their tithes and more to the church, never wanting to take advantage of the generosity of their unknown supporter. From time to time, someone would make an effort to breach the anonymity of the church's secret patron, but always without result.

This state of affairs continued for fourteen years. It was in August of 1904 that the rector of Saint Anthony's realized the annual gift upon which Saint Anthony's depended was late. The monies had always appeared in the church's account by the end of July. He thought it best to contact the solicitor and promptly sent a letter to the law firm in London. The response came not via post, but via rail. Two days later, a junior member of the firm who had not previously visited Newtown arrived on the afternoon train. He walked to the rector's residence, where he was invited in, and over a cup of tea explained the reason for his sudden appearance.

The young solicitor, who had recently been assigned to handle the matter, brought the rector two pieces of news. First, that a deposit to the church's account would shortly be made in the amount of fifteen thousand pounds. Second, this amount was coming to Saint Anthony's as a bequest per the anonymous donor's will and would be the final contribution the church would receive from its patron, who had passed away. The solicitor also made it clear that the donor had died some time ago but had left specific instructions that the final contribution be delayed until the present time.

The rector expressed profound gratitude for such a substantial gift to the church, though he also realized it would be the last. He thanked the solicitor for his firm's services over the years and for making the trip up from London. Then, for the first time ever, he made a slight effort toward learning the identity of the person who had been so generous for so long. "If you don't mind my asking," he said, "was the anonymous person ever known to me?" The solicitor smiled slightly and replied, "Rather well, I would say. And that is all I will say."

The solicitor left for London and the rector went into his study. He sat down behind his desk and picked up a pen, then put it down again. "I'll need to share this information at tomorrow's trustee meeting and pledge them to secrecy until Sunday," he said to himself. "Then, somehow I'll need to explain this to the people of the church. They will all want to know who the anonymous person was. And they will each try to figure it out. But I have the advantage."

The rector's assumption that on Sunday morning his parishioners would try to ascertain the identity of the church's anonymous benefactor was correct, but his timing was wrong. One or more of the trustees apparently could not resist the temptation to share this latest development, and soon the identity of the deceased patron became a popular topic in the community. Several people put forward theories on the topic and soon groups of like-minded individuals began to form. By Sunday morning, when the rector shared with his congregants the news about his recent visit with the solicitor, most had already heard multiple rumors and had already formed opinions about the anonymous benefactor's identity. Never had a Sunday message provoked such lively discussion and reluctance to leave the church grounds following the service.

Opinions regarding the likely identity of Saint Anthony's unknown patron varied considerably, and the citizens of Newtown were not reluctant to explain how they arrived at their conclusions and why others' ideas were incorrect. But, although a number of alleged identities were suggested, the field of posthumous candidates was soon narrowed based on several criteria. First was the obvious requirement that the anonymous person was no longer living. Also, the rector had shared the fact that the anonymous donor had died "some time ago" and the solicitor had been instructed to delay his final visit to Newtown. This was no doubt intended to help keep the person's identity shrouded in mystery.

The second criterion, which eliminated the bulk of the population, was the requirement to be of sufficient wealth to fund the donations the parish had received. This led to numerous assumptions about residents' incomes and assets, which resulted in a generally agreed upon list of nine possible contenders.

The first name that came to mind in terms of wealth was Lydia Ward, the widow of Neville Ward. When she inherited her husband's holdings, which consisted mainly of several large mines in the area, the estate was valued in the millions of pounds. But when the parishioners recalled that Mrs. Ward had argued vehemently against the Saint Anthony building project, calling it "a prideful waste" and "vainglorious as the Tower of Babel," they quickly eliminated her name from their lists.

The third criterion eliminated many of the remaining names. This was the necessity that the person in question not only held Saint Anthony's in high esteem but also possessed an empathetic nature sufficiently munificent to produce the extraordinary generosity demonstrated by the parish's anonymous supporter. In most people's view, only a few individuals could satisfy this criterion.

First to come to mind was Lord Arthur, the nobleman who had, when the new Saint Anthony's was first opened for public view, pledged one thousand pounds per year toward the building's upkeep. Although he did not live close to the village, he occasionally visited Newtown and made it a point to attend services at the church. He had also honored his promise of annual financial support without exception, until his death last year. What most villagers were not sure of was the degree of the gentleman's overall commitment to charity; was he a profound supporter of worthy causes or was his generosity to Saint Anthony's while living an uncommon act of charity?

A second possibility was Sir Richard Waltham, one of the wealthiest men in the entire region. Sir Richard had extensive holdings in the coal fields and owned large tracts of agricultural land. He was also known for his liberal contributions to several churches in the area. Some years ago he had completely funded construction of a new chapel in a town about 60 miles from Newtown. He was also suspected to be the source of donations made anonymously to two other churches and a nearby convent. He had visited Saint Anthony's on more than one occasion and expressed his great admiration for the church, and especially its pipe organ. In fact, it was the organ's sound that convinced Sir Richard to specify Saint Anthony's as the site of his funeral, held there earlier in the year. What was not known was whether his connection to Saint Anthony's was strong enough to motivate the level of funding contributed by the anonymous donor.

The third person villagers thought might be the secret benefactor was Edmund Brown, a Newtown native who had amassed a fortune in the shipping industry. Mr. Brown was seldom seen in the village, despite the fact that his aged parents lived there. But when he did visit, he always made a favorable impression on the villagers. He was outgoing, cordial, and, in the words of a local pub owner, "Ne'er acted as if his piles of pounds made him any diff'ent from the next bloke." Mr. Brown was also known to be exceptionally charitable, having contributed significant sums to hospitals, libraries, and churches in the region. His generosity continued unabated until his death some months ago. Granted, the records of Saint Anthony's Parish did not include significant contributions from Edmund Brown. But might he have done so anonymously?

A minority contingent of Newtown residents suggested a fourth possibility as the anonymous contributor, a woman named Elizabeth Wilson. Mrs. Wilson was the long-time widow of George Wilson, an industrialist and banker who was a leading citizen of Newtown until his death more than thirty years earlier. His widow was known for three things: her extreme piety and devotion to God and Saint Anthony's, her modest lifestyle, and her generosity to worthy causes. Although she preferred her giving to be anonymous, her contributions could not always be kept confidential, thus the citizens of Newtown were aware of sizeable donations Elizabeth Wilson had made to Saint Anthony's and other local institutions. She was highly regarded in the village, and the church was nearly filled when her funeral was held several months ago. However, there were at least two questions regarding the probability of Mrs. Wilson being the anonymous patron of Saint Anthony's. First, no one was certain of the extent of her inheritance or her current financial status, so her ability to donate the amounts received from the anonymous benefactor was unknown. Second, if Elizabeth Wilson was wealthy enough to be the anonymous donor, why would she publicly make sizeable donations to Saint Anthony's and at the same time secretly contribute more?

While the residents of Newtown pondered the mystery of the anonymous giver, the rector of Saint Anthony's was engaged in correspondence with the solicitor who now handled the matter. He explained that the parish trustees wanted to honor the person whose generosity had for many years kept the parish solvent and decided to do so by installing a bronze plaque at a prominent place in the church. The rector explained that the lengthy period of anonymous support had become an integral part of the history of Saint Anthony's and future generations deserved to know the full story of the magnificent edifice. Properly done, such recognition would, of course, include the name of the person to whom the church owed so much.

The young solicitor was not inclined to directly reveal the name of the anonymous donor. However, he was sympathetic to the rector's argument and in the course of their correspondence offered a few rather ambiguous hints as to the person's identity. They were enough. The rector was more familiar than most with the details of his parishioners' private lives. Through a careful process of elimination, he came to a firm conclusion regarding the identity of the person who for so long had remained anonymous.

The next Sunday, at the conclusion of the service, the rector motioned the organist not to begin the last hymn, and then addressed his congregation. "Before we sing this morning's recessional hymn," he began, "I want to put all of your minds at ease regarding a bit of a mystery that has enveloped our village for a long time." Those in the pews responded with silence and expectant expressions. The rector continued, "You are all aware of our desire to install a plaque that honors the individual who for years blessed our parish with tens of thousands of pounds of anonymous gifts -- the gifts that enabled so many people over so many years to see Saint Anthony's in all its splendor and majesty." The listeners were now totally focused on the rector, following each word carefully. "At another time I will explain in detail the precise process by which I have been able to determine the identity of the person in question. But for now, I will simply tell you that the plaque has been ordered, as the identity is no longer a mystery. And I will say one more thing after which the organist will commence our final hymn of the day. I will say only that, for nearly all of you, it was not who you think it was." The rector nodded toward the balcony, the organist summoned the mighty pipes to life, and the walls of Saint Anthony's reverberated with the beginning strains of the recessional hymn.

5

THE COPPER

I suppose it is common among the criminal class to blame someone else for their problems, irrespective of the likelihood that their own prior actions are responsible for their particular troubles. But if you understood the specifics of my own case, you would surely agree that the person accountable for my current predicament is not myself but my older brother Robert. Beginning in grammar school and continuing for over two decades, he educated me in the ways and methods of accumulating money by less than honest means.

Robert is the one whose example I followed when, as a youth, I learned how to shoplift by concealing items in large pockets added to the inside of my jacket. He taught me the importance of being observant of other people and their habits. He taught me how to identify a mark and deftly lift a wallet or other item from an unsuspecting person's pocket. My brother introduced me to his bookie, to the fences he used to convert stolen goods to pounds, and to a variety of unsavory people who used different names each time we met. And it was Robert who rescued me when, having failed to notice I was being observed by Harrod's security, I was pinched for shoplifting. My brother had a connection with a rather questionable member of the constabulary. By donating twenty-five pounds to a fictitious policemen's charity, Robert ensured that I avoided even a single night of incarceration.

Had my brother not intervened on my behalf, I likely would have been exposed to the unpleasant reality experienced by those arrested. Had I been incarcerated, the events which followed the Harrod's incident would almost certainly have been quite different. But by keeping me under his protective wing, Robert had granted me the opportunity to enjoy the rewards of illegitimate gain without bearing the associated risks. By this simple act of kindness, he set me on a path that was to lead inevitably to my present dilemma. Whether he would have taken the same action had he known the eventual result I cannot say. I only know that my current situation was avoidable, and I hold my brother accountable for it.

The skills I learned from my brother Robert were put to good use during several years of activity I refer to as my "career in unauthorized acquisitions." I was, if I say so myself, quite successful as an independent operator. I was highly observant and very logical, which enabled me to recognize opportunities and develop workable schemes. I had just the right balance between ambition and caution, sufficient initiative to pursue schemes that brought a fair income, but not so greedy as to engage in the types of high-risk behavior that had put many of my acquaintances in prison. I thought it wise to diversify my skill set and activities, and developed two rather lucrative schemes which elevated me beyond dependence on basic pickpocketing and shoplifting. I generally worked alone and preferred it that way, though one of my inventive schemes required the participation of a female partner.

The first scheme involved door-to-door sales of various household appliances and accessories. An acquaintance who worked in a printshop supplied the brochures, fictitious business cards, and order forms which I used during daytime at-home calls in residential neighborhoods. Each sale required a cash down payment of twenty percent, with the balance due upon delivery of the items ordered. I achieved a higher-than-expected success rate, though the total absence of deliveries prohibited repeat calls in the same area.

The second scheme required the participation of an attractive female, a sister of a bookie I knew. She would dress in an alluring outfit and sit alone in a bar in an upscale hotel. Soon she would be sipping a drink supplied by a man obviously not destitute and usually wearing a wedding band. I would wait in the lobby area close to the elevator, intently perusing a newspaper or magazine. My partner and her new acquaintance would soon pass through the lobby en route to the elevator. Passing by where I was sitting, she would discreetly drop a bar napkin.

A short time later, I would knock loudly on the door of the room number written on the napkin. The man who opened it would be shocked to encounter an enraged "husband," who fortunately, could be persuaded not to physically attack, sue, or report the man to the press or the police, provided sufficient cash changed hands. Those unfamiliar with men caught in a such situations would be surprised at the rapidity with which they will agree to a financial arrangement, and the amounts of money they are willing to part with.

Because I had not developed a taste for extravagant living, I was able to accumulate an impressive amount of savings. My brother Robert had warned me against holding too much in a single bank. In the event I ran afoul of the law, investigators would likely find out about the money I had on deposit, and explaining its source would be difficult at best. Although I did not relish the idea, I took my brother's advice and invested a few thousand pounds with a couple of his friends who were in the business of providing "unsecured personal loans" to individuals with pressing financial needs. Having provided the capital, I received one-third the interest charged, the other two-thirds being allocated to "administration" and "risk of non-payment."

Although my share of the profit charged for the loans was substantial, I withdrew from the arrangement when I learned that a high percentage of late-pay borrowers showed up on the lists of emergency room patients at the city hospitals. Instead, I placed modest amounts on deposit in a variety of banks in the greater London area. As a precaution, rather than use my full name, Arthur Clarke, I used my last name with various first names. I held bank accounts under names such as Alan Clarke, Alvin Clarke, Archie Clarke, Austin Clarke, and others.

For several years I had little contact with my older brother. Robert moved to East London and joined with some rather desperate blokes whose activities were too risky for me. He participated in numerous robberies, including a daring daytime heist at a jewelry store, and somehow got involved in an unsuccessful kidnapping scheme. He narrowly avoided a prison sentence and was allowed probation only because he had not been present when the kidnapping attempt took place. I preferred the less dramatic, but more reliable, activities I had been engaged in for some time, and enjoyed my comfortable and lower stress lifestyle.

All was well in my world, and I began to view myself as a respectable small businessman. I was never bothered by an uneasy conscience, probably because the only activities in which I engaged that produced sizeable sums of money were my hotel room visits to the men associating with my female partner, and they could clearly spare the funds. I occasionally heard from Robert, usually a brief phone call telling me about his latest "sure thing" with an expectation that I would be tempted to participate. I never felt the need and told him so. From time to time, he would call to describe yet another event his mates were planning, but he was seldom able to report a successful result.

Eventually, to my surprise, Robert separated from his mates and resumed the life of an independent operator. He had fulfilled his parole obligations and apparently the threat of prison had some effect on him. He appeared to have gotten over his tendency toward high-risk schemes and was careful about whom he associated with. We began to communicate regularly, and I was relieved that he did not press me to participate in any of his activities. He knew I was content with my career, and it seemed he was finally engaged in the types of endeavors at which he could be successful.

Over a period of about a year it became clear that Robert's abilities were best suited to planning and executing nighttime robberies of small businesses or middle-class homes. The security of such locations typically depended on standard door and window locks, and at most had basic security systems, many of which were not connected to an alarm service. Thus, gaining access was relatively simple, the items obtained were of a value easily fenced, and only two participants were required: one as entrant, and one as lookout/driver. My brother had found his niche, had a dependable assistant, and was steadily successful over a period of many months.

After years of friction between the two of us, I felt like Robert had finally gained some common sense. For the first time that I can recall we had a good relationship. I was happy for him and relieved that I no longer had to worry about his being involved in some high-risk scheme gone bad. He would often share his latest plan, and I sometimes contributed a minor suggestion intended to keep his risk at minimum. His assistant, whom I met only once, impressed me as reliable, observant, and —

most importantly – able to keep a confidence. My brother ran his business, I ran mine, and we respected our differences. In short, we got along like brothers should.

All went well for Robert and for me until about three years ago. Robert had shared a plan he concocted to acquire some valuable jewelry through a nighttime visit to a well-known retail establishment in Camden. As usual, I had helped with logistical planning and suggested a reliable fence who could dispose of the goods. The plan was well thought out and the street value of the items targeted exceeded thirty thousand pounds, an amount considerably greater than usual. The jewelry store had been thoroughly cased, and Robert's assistant was in possession of a wiring schematic of the building's alarm system. I wished my brother well and looked forward to hearing about another successful heist.

The afternoon of the planned robbery I received a call from Robert. He apologized for intruding but was desperately in need of help. His assistant had, without my brother's knowledge, begun to augment his income by serving as motorman for a small group operating in the area around Islington. Their schemes were opportunistic and typically involved obviously well-to-do tourists or other foreigners. When members of the group completed an acquisition of cash or other valuables, my brother's assistant provided rapid transportation from the scene. Unfortunately, the evening before my brother called to ask for help, an unexpected traffic jam had left his assistant in the hands of pursuing police.

Robert explained the predicament he was in, reiterated the scope of the opportunity before him, and solicited my participation. I pondered the situation, reminding myself that I had consistently denied his previous attempts to involve me in his schemes. But I had to admit the current plan was sound and the potential reward was impressive. So I reluctantly agreed to help my brother in his time of need. I was to precede him to the site, disable the alarm system, and ensure the building was not occupied. After an agreed length of time, I would return in a rental car, collect my brother, and deposit him at the door of the designated fence.

Our plan had proven to be impeccable. The alarm schematic was accurate, my brother entered and exited the building without incident, and we drove off with satchels containing jewelry certain to fund our living expenses for months to come. We parted in a self-congratulatory mood. I returned the rental car and took the tube to the station nearest my home, where I enjoyed a leisurely nightcap while reflecting on the evening's events. I expected that within a few weeks at most I would receive a nondescript parcel containing a significant amount of cash, which I would then deposit in one of the banks where I held my accounts.

It is a gratifying thing to observe the unfolding of a carefully constructed plan. It is equally gratifying to stand at the teller window of a bank and deposit the results of such a plan, which is exactly what I did about three weeks later. As I exited the bank, there was a spring in my step and a feeling of contentment that was not usual for me. Ever observant, including of my own behaviors, I realized my mood was elevated by a combination of financial gain and having engaged in a joint venture with my brother. I expect Robert had similar feelings. Unfortunately, our elation was short-lived.

I had made the deposit at a branch bank in Kensington. As a precaution, to ensure I remained anonymous, I left my car at home and took the tube. I walked from the station to the bank, deposited the money, and walked back to the station. I rode the tube back to my station, exited and walked home. I unlocked the door and went into the house, hung up my jacket, and went into my office. I took the bank receipt out of my pocket and put it in the left drawer of my desk. I went into the kitchen and began brewing a pot of tea when the doorbell rang. As was my habit, I peered out of the office curtain and saw two men in suits at the front door.

As I went to the door, I had a bad feeling. My business associates, including bookies, fences, and my female partner, never came to my house. And when we met to discuss business, they came alone. I couldn't recall any reason two men would appear unannounced at my home. It occurred to me they might have the wrong address, but I discarded that idea. As I opened the door, the taller of the two men spoke. "Mr. Arthur Clarke?" he asked. "Yes," I said. "What can I do for you?" The man held up an ID badge, introduced himself and the man accompanying him, and invited himself in. I told the men I was making tea and asked if they wanted a cup. They accepted my offer, and, without being asked, sat down in my front room next to the fireplace.

Who was the author who wrote, "The best laid schemes of mice and men ..."? For certain, the scheme laid down by Robert and me was one of the best I'd seen. There was nothing wrong with the plan. The only flaw, of which I was not aware prior to the two men's visit to my home, was the fact that my brother and I were not the only ones who knew about the plan. Since Robert's assistant was originally designated as the wheelman, he knew every detail. And, when he was so ignominiously removed from circulation after being detained in the unexpected traffic jam, he proved to be of weaker character than we had thought. Under pressure from the police, and at the advice of a hastily retained solicitor, he had bargained away the details of our plan in exchange for leniency.

As the two strangers sat sipping my tea and explaining the events that led them to investigate my assorted bank accounts, I was surprised that my reaction was not one of anger toward Robert's assistant for betraying our confidence, nor toward my brother for drawing me into the activity which it now appeared could be my undoing. The logical aspect of my nature prevailed. Robert and I had in fact followed a perfectly viable plan, and his assistant had only done what most men might do when presented an opportunity to improve the consequences of their actions. I recognized the reality of my situation, and as the men plied me with questions, I calmly and logically explained the nature of our plan, the care with which it had been developed, and the expected result. I stopped short of naming the fence involved. My visitors seemed appreciative of my candor and did not pursue the issue of how the acquired jewelry was converted to cash.

I expected to be arrested, possibly handcuffed, and transported to the nearest police station. Instead, the taller man stood and said, "Is there a room where I can make a phone call?" I nodded toward the library. He walked into the room and closed the door. A few minutes later, he reappeared and resumed his seat by the fireplace. "If you don't mind," he said, "Might there be another spot of tea? We're going to be here a while until DCI Madsen arrives." The other man raised his eyebrows but said nothing. "Tea for you also?" I asked. "Oh, yes, please," he replied. I went to the kitchen, brewed a fresh pot of tea, and rejoined the two men.

The shorter man brought his cup to his lips, took a sip, and said, "A fine cuppa, this is." "East India Black," I said, smiling slightly. "I'm glad it's to your liking." The taller man silently sipped his tea while looking intently at me. After a couple of minutes, he spoke. "We have had our eye on you for some time, Mr. Clarke. We know far more about you than you might think. Your pickpocketing, your shoplifting – I'd guess this tea came from Harrod's, no charge -- your door-to-door sales of phantom goods, your little hotel visits. Even the name of the fence you used for the jewelry heist, which is why we didn't press you on the matter."

For the second time that afternoon, I had a feeling of considerable unease. I didn't like where the conversation was heading. Just when I was beginning to feel discouraged, the tall man resumed speaking. "When DCI Madsen arrives," he said sternly, "I'm quite sure he's going to offer you an extraordinary opportunity. I'd suggest that if the offer is made, you latch on to it with enthusiasm." I had no idea what the man was talking about. But in my usual manner I paid careful attention to what he said, as well as the reaction of the other man, who was frowning and nodding his head up and down. Just then, the doorbell rang.

Instead of peering out the window from behind a curtain as I normally did, I went directly to the front door and opened it. The man I faced did not meet my expectation regarding the appearance of a detective chief inspector. He was short, impeccably dressed, and wore a pleasant expression. He extended his hand and asked, "May I presume you are Mr. Arthur Clarke?" His mannerisms seemed more that of a salesman than a policeman. I nodded, briefly shook the man's hand and gestured toward the room where his fellow constables waited. With a slight smile, he motioned for me to precede him, followed me into the room, and stood waiting for an invitation to have a seat. I pointed to an empty chair, and he sat down. I offered tea, which he declined by saying, "Sorry, I don't mean to be rude, but I don't want to put you to any trouble at all. And my time is very limited."

I was having major misgivings about DCI Madsen. Based on the man's conduct, an observer might have thought he was an old friend who dropped by for a casual visit. I found his behavior disconcerting and wished he were more like a typical London constable. My wish was granted when the inspector resumed the conversation. "I shall be direct," he said, no longer smiling. "Without question we have enough evidence to ensure you exchange this very pleasant address for a cell in Brixton or Pentonville, which is precisely what you deserve. However, I've been assigned to head up what some of my colleagues refer to as a barmy turnabout experiment. In short, here's my offer."

My curiosity was piqued and I listened intently to DCI Madsen. "Frankly, Clarke," he continued, "we need a more effective way of curtailing the increasing number of mid-level property crimes, especially in the affluent suburbs." I was well aware of the preponderance of robberies to which the inspector referred, and I understood why he felt pressure to reverse the trend. But I wasn't sure where the conversation was headed. The inspector pulled his chair closer to mine. "Whether you admit it or not, you know numerous people involved in this type of criminality, at least on the periphery, and how they operate. And we know you are intelligent, logical, and observant – abilities we believe are key to putting a stop to the current rash of robberies."

I said nothing, but silently agreed with what the man had said. DCI Madsen leaned forward, his face just inches from my own. "Here's my offer," he said. "You use your skills and contacts to help us solve our little problem and we forget about prosecuting you. That's it, period." The inspector settled back in his chair and relaxed, but his expression remained stern. "You will have a few days to think it over," he continued. "Yes and you're scot-free, no and you're sent down. Any questions?"

It took me only a few seconds to digest what the inspector had said. "So," I asked, "you want me to be an informant?" DCI Madsen's smile returned. "Not at all," he said. "We want you to join the force." I was more than surprised. "You want me to be a copper?" I asked, incredulously. "Correct," the inspector said. "Although I don't care for the term. We'll provide a story to cover your background, give you required training, and assign you to a special team. You stay in line, do what we ask, and in a few years your record is scrubbed clean." "How many years?" I asked. "Probably no less than three, no more than five," the inspector replied. "We'll know by then how well this approach works. But the choice is yours."

I thought about where I lived, how I lived, and what enabled me to maintain my standard of living. I thought about what I had heard about life in prison, and what people faced when released. I thought about my brother, and wondered what Robert would do in the same circumstance. As I was pondering what I had heard, DCI Madsen stood up, which led the other two men to stand. He drew a business card from his pocket and handed it to me. With a smile, he offered me his hand and said, "I need to go, and you have a decision to make. Call my mobile within the week." Then his smile disappeared. "Just remember," he said, "You keep your end of the bargain, we keep ours. You don't, and your friends can come to visit you once a week for a few years. Don't slip up. We'll let ourselves out." With his two colleagues in tow, DCI Madsen exited the house, leaving me to finish my tea while I replayed in my mind everything he had said.

Three days later, I called DCI Madsen and informed him of my decision. In just a couple of minutes of what seemed to me like a surreal conversation, I told him I intended to accept his offer. His only words were, "Right decision. We'll be in touch. Don't leave London until you hear from us." So that was that. After years of success as a lone operator, never having to answer to anyone, I had just agreed to join an organization that had many of the characteristics of a military force, including an obligation to obey the orders of whoever was placed above me. I asked myself how this unfortunate situation could have possibly happened to me. Then I realized it was the result of a long series of events that traced back to my youth, to when I first learned the skills of my trade from my older brother.

Anyone who knew me well would not have been surprised at my decision. My career was proof of my risk-averse nature, as well as my penchant for working and living independently. It would have been totally illogical to refuse the offer of clemency in favor of a prison term, even though accepting the terms offered by DCI Madsen would require me to act in ways incompatible with my beliefs regarding wealth, fairness, and pragmatism. Also, anyone familiar with my upbringing would realize that the person ultimately responsible for my situation – the person who had set me on the path that led to the predicament I currently faced -- was my brother Robert.

Following the call informing DCI Madsen of my decision, I was curious about how well I would get on with my new mates. Initially, there were some awkward moments. One occurred just a week after my decision, during my orientation to the police force. Though this would normally be left to someone of lower rank, DCI Madsen toured me around the division office and introduced me to his staff. I recognized one chap, and later remarked to Madsen, "I knew the fellow in the third office. He's the bloke you had tail me after you told me not to leave London until I made my decision." The inspector frowned, then broke into a broad smile. "Well," he said, "I guess we were spot on about your acute powers of observation. Don't worry, you'll have plenty of opportunity to keep them honed here."

My first assignment, on which I was partnered with another detective for nearly four months, was routine and boring. The two of us were assigned to follow up leads submitted in response to newspaper ads promising rewards for arrests related to incidents involving fraud. The two of us shared work that could easily have been done by one man, which in my first experience as a public employee I took as an example of government inefficiency. In retrospect, I realize the other detective was there to monitor my activities and to keep DCI Madsen informed of my progress. Fortunately, there was nothing to report that went beyond the bounds of the agreement that ensured my freedom.

I had largely disconnected myself from my former business associates, including the woman with whom I had partnered for the hotel scheme. I had no contact with any fence, motorman, engraver, or other service provider. After the jewelry store incident – the one that had led to DCI Madsen's visit to my home -- my brother and I had decided not to undertake any additional joint ventures. But I also wanted to avoid the embarrassment I would face if he learned of my new occupation. During a phone conversation, I invented a story about an acquaintance being nicked due to a phone tap and told him I thought the police might have a way to listen in on our conversations. Robert readily agreed we ought to cease all communication, at least for the foreseeable future. This saved me from having to lie to him about what I was doing and protected him from the abuse his associates would subject him to if they heard about my new position.

I adapted to police work rather rapidly and concluded that DCI Madsen had shown admirable insight when he chose to recruit me. During my first two years on the force, I was credited with nineteen arrests for swindling and thirteen for fraud. I received a promotion from special constable to detective sergeant and an increase in salary, which was appreciated since I had found it necessary to adjust my lifestyle to align with a decrease in income. The bank accounts the police discovered had been frozen, though they did not include a sizeable sum I had entrusted to an acquaintance outside the London metropolis. However, utilizing any appreciable amount of such funds would have undoubtedly raised suspicions so they remained untouched.

My unexpected career in law enforcement proved quite successful, and I rapidly assumed greater responsibilities. My experience proved highly valuable, though I was careful to avoid citing specific experiences as illustrations of the methods we were attempting to curtail. I was busy and productive, and I truly did not regret cutting ties with my old associates. It bothered me somewhat that I let my brother believe I was still engaged in the same activities which had long been my support, but there would simply be no benefit to letting Robert in on my clandestine arrangement with DCI Madsen.

As a member of the London police force, I fully applied my abilities and advanced with exceptional rapidity. After just over three years, I had attained the rank of detective inspector and was put in charge of a task force charged with reducing property crimes in the Greenwich Park area. The heists appeared to be the work of a well-organized, sizeable organization, and represented the type of persistent issue that had led to the experimental program of which I was a part. Some residents of the area were politically connected, and pressure to solve the issue was being felt by the higher-ups in the police force. About six weeks after I was put in charge of the special group, I was summoned to a meeting in division headquarters. When I arrived for the meeting, I was surprised to find the only other attendee was DCI Madsen.

The inspector offered a cordial greeting, asked if I wanted tea, and invited me to sit down. He seemed more relaxed than usual. We visited while sipping our tea, though not about anything consequential, and I wondered about the purpose of our meeting. After a few more minutes of casual banter, DCI Madsen leaned back in his chair and said, "I've been carefully following your task force and I like what you've done. But it's not enough to satisfy City Hall." I sensed a disconnect between the compliment he had just offered and the mention of dissatisfied politicians. All I could do was wait for DCI Madsen to give me more information.

The inspector continued, "When we finish our conversation, you will be joined by two men who have been working undercover in support of this project. I didn't tell you about them because you didn't need to know. They have achieved a breakthrough of major proportion, which they will review with you. When you have gone over their information, come up to my office and we'll lay out the next steps. Is that clear?" I nodded. "Oh, and one other thing," the inspector said. "When this task force is successful, we're going to consider this entire project a success. That means we will purge your arrest record and unfreeze your bank accounts, as promised. Whether you remain with the force after that is up to you." Then, he rose and left the room.

My mind was entertaining several thoughts at once. Why the secrecy? Was it a sign I really was not trusted? Why weren't the undercover men there the same time as DCI Madsen? Why wasn't new information simply sent to me through normal channels? Why would he insist on being part of planning next steps, when he knew I was capable? What was the breakthrough? Why was it significant enough to be the deciding point of whether the experiment was a success? Exactly where and how had the undercover men ....

My thoughts were interrupted by two men entering the meeting room. They were dressed in casual clothes and were not freshly shaven. The shorter of the two had a prominent tattoo on his left forearm and a smaller one on the right side of his neck. The taller man held a large brown folder labeled "GP12". The men sat down, introduced themselves, and began to review the contents of the folder. The undercover men had infiltrated a loosely affiliated group of motormen, fences, and other people relied on by those carrying out the heists in Greenwich Park. But rather than arresting these minor players, they had continued their involvement and built sufficient trust to learn the identities of the two men in charge of the operation. It was now time to find and arrest them.

The plan concocted by DCI Madsen was simple but required careful coordination. At a given time just a few days in the future, the undercover men would verify the location of each of the two ringleaders. Then, two teams of three men each would simultaneously arrest the two ringleaders. DCI Madsen would lead one team and I would lead the other. For reasons he did not share, the inspector would make the decision regarding which team pursued which of the two suspects just prior to the agreed time of arrest. Backup for each team would be provided; that was none of my concern. My responsibility was to ensure my team made a swift, sure, clean arrest of our assigned target without giving an anticipated solicitor of the person arrested any possible cause to assert police abuse or improper procedure.

Early on the evening that was selected for the pinch, both teams met in DCI Madsen's office at division headquarters. The inspector went over the plan, which I thought unnecessary. He asked if we had any questions, which none of us did. Then he asked the other four men to leave the office so he could have a private word with me. As soon as we were alone, he said, "I'm giving you the name and address of the one your team is to bring in." As he spoke, he handed me a half-sheet of paper on which were written a man's name and a street address. I read the information, looked the inspector directly in the eye, and said, "Got it." DCI Madsen called the other men back into his office. Twelve minutes later, his mobile phone rang. He answered it and said, "Are you absolutely certain?" He terminated the call, turned to us, and said, "It's a go."

A short time later, I and the other two men on my team pulled up across the street from a high-end apartment building. We got out of our unmarked car and walked across the street to the building's entrance. A uniformed doorkeeper stood just outside the large glass entrance doors. I flashed my badge and said, "Police business. Don't let anyone else in until we come out." The doorkeeper's eyes widened as he opened the door and said, "Yes, sir." I led the other two men into the lobby, walked quickly to the elevator and pushed the button. The door opened, and as we entered the elevator I pushed button number seven. One of the men said, "That's ironic. Probably the guy's lucky number." The elevator started ascending.

When we got off the elevator, one of my team members said, "I think you forgot to tell us this bloke's name. What's on that paper Madsen gave you?" I showed both men the paper, then led them down the hall to apartment 707. I rang the doorbell and waited, remaining directly in front of the peephole in the door. We heard the door lock turn, then the doorknob, and the door opened. A man opened the door. He was about my height, well-dressed and carefully groomed. He surveyed the scene, giving a quick glance at each of the other men on my team, and sounded mildly surprised as he asked, "Yes, what is it?" I looked him in the eye and said, "Robert Clarke, you are under arrest. You do not have to say anything, but it may harm your defense if you do not mention when questioned something which .... ". The man under arrest interrupted me. "Yes, I know the speech," he said. He held out his hands, and one of my men handcuffed him. He pulled the apartment door shut and said, "You wouldn't have needed the cuffs. Let's go, little brother."

6

THE DOCTOR

It was difficult to tell which man was more tired, the physician or the young man at the wheel of his car. The doctor had gone virtually without sleep for over two weeks before his wife convinced him to hire a driver.

"You won't be any good to anybody if you keep up like this," Althea Carter had told her husband. "And if you end up sick in bed, who am I going to call?" Franklin Carter had reluctantly accepted his wife's advice and secured the services of Thomas Miller, a local handyman who had little work in the winter. With someone else driving his several year-old Model T, Doctor Carter could nap between house calls, enabling him to maintain the taxing schedule that began with the start of the flu epidemic.

Thomas Miller's house was just across the street and one house down from the Carter home. It was Mrs. Carter's idea to put a candle in the front window of their house when the driver's services were needed. Day or night, Mrs. Carter would answer the phone, and based on a brief conversation with the caller, determine whether the doctor needed to be roused to visit a patient. If her husband happened to be at home and the reported situation merited, she would light the candle, ready the doctor's bag and place his heavy coat, fur hat, gloves and galoshes near the front door. Only when she saw the Model T in front of the house with the engine running would she wake her husband, who had often dozed off in a chair in the sitting room.

The few hours Thomas Miller was home he slept on the sofa in the front room while his wife kept watch toward the Carter house. When she saw the lighted candle in their front window, she would wake her husband. Since the Millers had a garage but no car, the doctor's car was kept at the Millers. At the signal of the lighted candle, Mr. Miller would put on his winter outerwear and go to the garage, where he would follow the intricate procedure required to start the Model T in cold weather.

Mr. Miller would begin by sitting in the driver's seat and pressing each of the foot pedals to squeeze oil out from between the transmission plates. (Failure to do so would allow the plates to drag enough to propel the car when it started.) He adjusted the levers on the steering column to retard the spark and minimize the throttle. He would open the hood to turn on the fuel, then move to the front and pull the choke wire. Using his left hand and keeping his thumb out of the way, he would prime the fuel by cranking the engine over three times, then release the choke. He would reach into the car to turn on the ignition, return to the front and again crank the engine, hoping it would come to life.

Once the Model T was running, Thomas Miller would pull it up in front of the Carter house. The doctor would get in and announce their destination, which was typically the first of several to be visited, and the two men would drive off into the cold. After a snowstorm, theirs was often the first vehicle on the road, its narrow tires breaking a path through the white, frigid drifts. Daytime travel was uncomfortably cold but manageable. The most arduous forays were made after dark when falling snow or wind made visibility tenuous at best. Although he hated to do so, Thomas sometimes had to ask his fatigued passenger to remain awake and watch for the edge of the road. Many times, when the two weary men finally arrived back at the Carters' house, the doctor's wife met them with news of yet another patient requesting they come at once.

This routine was repeated time and again during the long, cold winter. Experts predicted that cold weather would bring relief, but the Spanish flu seemed to be an exception to the normal seasonal pattern. Young and old alike contracted the flu, and although some patient outcomes exceeded the doctor's expectations, for many the disease proved fatal.

As the only physician in the area, the burden of caring for the epidemic's victims fell solely on Dr. Carter. His wife screened the calls as carefully as possible, but the majority resulted in yet another trip across town or into the countryside. Without so much as a respite for Christmas, the doctor and his driver toiled on through the long months of winter. Neither man saw the other's commitment and sacrifice as exceptional or even worthy of comment. They simply kept on, day after day, night after night, doing what needed to be done.

Most of Dr. Carter's patients were far from wealthy, and many had difficulty paying for his services. The loss of income caused by a protracted illness could bring financial disaster on a family, even without trying to pay for doctor and medicine bills. Yet, his patients did their best to compensate the physician for the care he provided. It was not uncommon for the doctor and his driver to return to town with the rear seat of the Model T filled with home-baked pie or other dessert, canned goods, eggs, or handiwork. Mrs. Carter used only what was needed from these provisions, distributing the rest to the poor in the community.

Working together for long hours and in trying circumstances can bring out the worst in people. It would not have been surprising if Dr. Franklin Carter and Mr. Thomas Miller had, after months of their grueling schedule, had a falling out, or at least an occasional argument. Perhaps it was their focus on the task at hand and their sympathy for those with whom they came in contact that allowed them to remain in good humor and avoid complaining or quarrelling. Whatever the reason, when asked years later about his experience as Dr. Carter's driver during the flu epidemic, Mr. Miller could recall only a single instance when the two men had a genuine disagreement, but he remembered the incident distinctly.

It was in the very late winter or early spring of '19. The weather was clear, and the temperature had risen from below freezing to nearly forty degrees. Snow had begun to melt, turning farmyards and the roads leading to them into muddy quagmires. Travel by automobile was transformed from a rough ride over frozen ground to a struggle to coax the Model T onward through mud and muck. Thomas Miller did his absolute best to deliver Dr. Carter to his awaiting patients as quickly as possible, including cutting across still-frozen field to avoid low spots in the roads and fitting a bracket to the front bumper of the Model T to which a team of horses could be hitched when the doctor's car was hopelessly mired in the mud.

The thaw lasted about two weeks, by which time both the Model T and its passengers had nearly reached the limits of their capacities for dealing with soupy roads and mud-crusted clothing. Then it froze again, casting the ruts and clumps of mud into solid rock-hard barriers that tested the car's durability and the men's patience with every mile. After one particularly stressful sixteen-hour day of bouncing over potholes and ruts, the driver and the doctor arrived back in town feeling drained and peevish.

As they pulled up in front of the doctor's residence, Mrs. Carter emerged from the house and walked rapidly to the car. "Don't shut it off or get out," she said. "I've another urgent call." The two men in the car looked at each other, communicating their feelings without speaking. The doctor sighed and spoke. "All right, Althea," he said, "who is it and what do they want?" Mrs. Carter's expression was one of sympathy for the two tired men. "It's Mrs. Humphrey again," she said. "Her daughter-in-law called and said she's taken a turn for the worse. She said her mother-in-law asked for you." Mrs. Carter noticed the expression on the driver's face and added, "Sorry, Thomas, I know you're really tired and hungry." The driver responded, "It's up to Doc. I go if he goes." Mrs. Carter smiled weakly and offered, "How about I quickly make a couple of sandwiches for you to take along?" Her husband nodded. "Guess we're going, then," said the driver.

A few moments later, the two men were heading back out of town in the direction from which they had just come. The driver, who was pushing the Model T a bit harder than usual, glanced at the doctor and said, "I don't think I know this one. A Mrs. Humphrey?" The doctor shook his head. "They don't get to town often. They live out past Hiram Kammer's place about five miles." The driver scowled. "Five miles past Kammer's?" he asked. "Franklin, but do we really need to go way out there right now?" The doctor looked off toward the horizon. "Yes, Tom," he said. "we do." The driver shook his head side to side, pursed his lips, and pulled on the Model T's throttle lever. The car bounced along the frozen ground, the doctor's bag shifting from side to side in the back seat. The doctor hoped his well-used car would hold up to such treatment but said nothing.

An hour later the doctor pointed ahead and said to the driver, "Tom, turn right at this corner; the Kammer place is on top the hill." At the corner, the driver began to turn right, then stopped, backed up and drove through the intersection. "Your transmission bands are worn," he said. "I'll have to back up the hill." With that, he pushed the reverse pedal, turned the car, and began to steer it toward the hill. The car bounced over the frozen ruts, then slowed as the hill steepened. "I'm not sure about this," said the driver, "but I'll try." He pulled the throttle down for more speed, but the increasing slope of the hill prevented the car from accelerating.

The hill was nearly half a mile long, and the car made it two-thirds of the way to the top before the passengers smelled something hot. Then steam began to pour from the radiator cap. "This is as far as we're going, Franklin," said Tom. "We'll have to let it cool a while, then maybe try some more." The doctor shook his head. "We don't have that kind of time, Tom," he said. "We'll have to walk up the rest of the way. You can get some water from the Kammers." The doctor stepped out of the car, retrieved his bag from the back seat, and turned to face uphill. For the first time ever, the driver held back. "This better be a life saver," he said. "We've probably damaged the car and won't do ourselves any good either." The doctor did not reply but began his trek up the hill.

When the two men reached the farmhouse, they were welcomed by Mrs. Humphrey's daughter-in-law. "Grandma's upstairs in her bedroom," she said. "She' been waiting for you." Bag in hand, the doctor ascended the stairs. The woman who had let them in addressed the driver. "Bet you're tired out, eh Tom?" she asked. "Sit down here at the table and I'll get you a slice of pie and a cup of coffee." The driver smiled slightly and sat down in an upright wooden chair. The chair had at one time displayed a painted design, but the paint was long worn away. The table matched the chair. The driver had eaten most of the piece of pie and drunk half of his coffee when he dozed off, his head braced by an arm that rested precariously on one elbow.

"Are you ready, Tom?" the doctor asked. The driver shook his head to clear the fogginess of his sleep. "Huh? Oh, sure," he said, and got up from the table. "Thank you, ma'am, for the food," he said. The woman smiled. "Thank both of you for coming so soon," she replied. "Charles is out in the yard getting the water for your car. You can bring the bucket back next time you come." The doctor shook the woman's hand, and the men left the house. A man crossed the yard with a bucket of water and gave it to the driver, who carried it down the hill to the waiting Model T. The engine had cooled, and the driver removed the radiator cap and poured in the water. He set the spark, turned on the ignition, grasped the crank and brought the car to life.

Neither man spoke as the automobile bounced and rattled down the hill. After they had reached the bottom and turned back toward town, the driver spoke. "Usually after we leave a patient," he said, "you tell me what you did and how they're doing." The doctor did not respond. "I'm curious," said the driver. "Why not this time?" There was a short period of silence, after which the doctor spoke. "Because there is not much to say," he said. "Mrs. Humphrey is not going to survive the flu. I knew that the last time I was here, when her son-in-law fetched me with his horse and wagon. And she knew it, too. She'll probably not last through tomorrow."

The driver furrowed his brow. "Are you telling me, Franklin," he began, his voice increasing in volume. "Are you telling me that after we made it back to town dog tired and half frozen that we turned around and came all the way out here so you could see a woman you knew was going to die anyway?" "That's right, Tom," the doctor replied. "Well, why in tarnation would we do a fool thing like that?" the driver demanded, and added, "and you probably won't get paid for it, either!"

The doctor spoke softly. "Tom," he said, "in the midst of this terrible epidemic, with friends and neighbors dying all around them, you and I are the only hope these people have. And they have to know that when they call for help, someone will come."

The men rode the rest of the way back to town in silence; the doctor lapsed in and out of sleep. The driver steered the car to the center of town and turned down his home street. He pulled up in front of the doctor's house. The doctor stepped out of the car, grabbed his bag, and said, "Thanks for what you're doing, Tom. Not just for me, but for them. I hope you understand." The driver looked at his passenger. He thought just a moment and said, "Just put the candle in the window." He pushed on the floor pedal, gripped the wheel, and steered the Model T toward home.

7

THE HEIST

The town of Blue Springs, like other western towns, was founded by a speculator who bought barren land, drew up a grandiose plan for a future city, and promoted the town as "the next Saint Louis." The town never grew to more than six hundred people and might have disappeared altogether except for its fortuitous location. More through luck than foresight, it was located at what was to become the intersection of an east-west rail line and a north-south line. It was also the nearest town to Fort Larned, and as such became the source of local supplies and the terminus of army shipments to the fort. Proximity to the fort, which was staffed with two full companies of soldiers, ensured the town's survival and the presence of four unusual attributes.

Despite the town's small size, Blue Springs boasted of a larger than expected retail establishment, an impressive bank building, and a sizeable railroad depot. The growth of Perkins General Store was attributed to the combined needs of the area's ranchers and farmers plus the short-term requirements of Fort Larned. The depot, whose property included a cattle corral, was built to accommodate supply shipments to the fort and to handle the transfer of freight and cattle between the two rail lines that met at Blue Springs. The large volume of railroad business and retail trade created the need for a bank beyond that normally expected in a small community.

One other unusual attribute of Blue Springs, though not of major impact, was the fact that the local sheriff had five deputies, a remarkable number for a town of a few hundred people. The explanation was simple. The five men were deputized solely to guard the monthly payroll shipments to Fort Larned and were only on duty the days the payrolls arrived in Blue Springs or were transported from the local bank to the fort. Although there had never been any problem with the payroll shipments, the amount of money involved was sizeable and the sheriff believed a visible contingent of armed guards would discourage anyone from attempting to interfere with the transfer of the payroll between the depot, the bank, and the fort. The bank president, who had in his younger years worked in law enforcement back east, appreciated and supported the sheriff's cautious approach.

About fifteen miles from Blue Springs, along a creek which flowed into the Pawnee River, sat an empty cabin nestled among a stand of elm, ash, and cottonwood trees. It was an isolated location, at one time the home of a recluse trapper named Beaver Bill, but long since abandoned. As naturally happens with empty structures, the cabin had deteriorated over time. But it could still shelter the unfortunate soul caught in the area by a sudden storm, or having failed to reach their destination by nightfall, requiring temporary refuge. Had such a traveler reached the cabin during a certain period during the fall of sixty-seven, they would have been surprised to find it occupied by a group of men. And had they been familiar with the wanted posters circulated in the area at the time, they might have recognized some of the cabin's occupants.

Five men were holed up in the cabin, their horses hidden in the woods beside the creek. They had ridden together for more than three years, perpetrating a string of robberies primarily involving trains or banks. As was common among such malefactors, they knew little of each other's backgrounds and only addressed each other by their given names. The leader of the gang, a tall, pock-faced man named Jesse, was a meticulous planner who disliked risk and tolerated no deviance from his detailed instructions. Two of the gang, Russell and Frank, were brothers who had worked as ranch hands until they found it more profitable to steal cattle than to raise them. They gave up rustling after nearly being caught and joined Jesse, believing his methods offered a greater chance of wealth with less chance of hanging. The other two men, Reed and Cooper, were drifters who joined Jesse on a whim but had learned much from the man and were intensely loyal to him.

The five men had been staying in the cabin for nearly three weeks while Jesse crafted a plan to relieve the U.S. Army of its burdensome payroll on its way to Fort Larned. The other men were trying to be patient, fully aware that the scheme their leader concocted would have a high probability of success with minimal risk. But they were also eager for activity and concerned their presence in the abandoned cabin might be discovered. Though feeling restless, the four listened attentively while Jesse laid out his strategy. They knew every phase of the operation would be described in detail and they would be expected to remember and implement each step precisely as directed.

"Cooper, you and Reed have been in Blue Springs three times," Jesse began. "You know all we need to, cause I don't want nobody in town from now until we hit the bank. Too much chance of bein' recognized." The other men nodded their agreement. "Now," Jesse continued, "lay it out for us, slow and careful like." Reed began. "The army payroll comes on the afternoon train the last Thursday of the month; that's in two days. It gits from the depot to the bank on a wagon with four deputies ridin' 'long side. Goes in the bank vault till Friday 'bout noon. Friday afternoon, army wagon with a whole mess a' troopers comes to git it."

The men thought for a moment about what they had just heard. Then Russell said, "Could hit the train this side a Blue Springs. No point tryin' to git it away from the army." "Right about the army," said Jesse, "but the train has guards, too. Only one way. We hit the bank Friday mornin'." Jesse nodded toward Cooper. "Tell 'em 'bout the bank," he said. "And listen careful," Jesse added, " 'cause Cooper don't miss nuthin'."

Cooper began his report. "Bank opens at eight; mebbe a minute or two late. President and one teller in there alone until nine. Then a clerk, one guard and 'nother teller show up. Then they open the vault."

"So," Russell asked, "hit it right away Friday mornin'?" Cooper did not respond. The men all looked toward Jesse. "Fifteen after eight," he said, "gives us forty-five minutes." Frank frowned, "But the vault's locked," he said. Jesse ignored Frank's comment and turned his attention toward Cooper, a sign he should continue.

"The president opens the vault. And with a little encouragement, he'll do it early," Cooper said. The other men chuckled. Cooper continued, "Come in the door, there's two teller windows straight on. Corner to the right's a hat rack, umbrella holder, and chair the guard sits in."

"He won't be there at eight," interjected Frank.

"Fifteen after," said Jesse, scowling at Frank.

"I know," said Frank, "I was just sayin'..." His words trailed off when he noticed Jesse's expression.

Cooper resumed his report. "Left hand corner there's a clock on the wall, ten minutes slow. Neath the clock's some boxes sayin' 'bank records' and next to them two round-backed chairs fer waitin'. Behind the teller windows, two desks, one for the clerk 'n the other empty. The back wall left of the clerk a door to the president's office. Between the desks a pot-bellied stove, a pail a coal, and a wooden cabinet 'bout four feet tall and three feet wide."

"I told you he don't miss nothin'," Jesse said, without irony. Jesse turned to Reed and said, "Tell 'em 'bout behind the bank." Reed nodded. "Good setup," he said, "some kinda shed 'bout half the width of the bank. Other side there's a back door comes outa the president's office and a hitchin' post right there. Good place to have our horses waitin'." The other men liked what they heard.

"Should be easy," Frank said.

Jesse glowered at Frank. "There ain't no such thing," he said, quietly but with a steely expression. "The man who thinks takin' a bank is easy is the one who dies tryin' it."

Frank's face flushed. "I just meant …" He didn't finish the sentence.

"Here's what we do," Jesse said, no longer concerned with Frank's misstatement. "Friday mornin', we hitch up behind the bank just after eight. Frank and Russell go 'round the front door. You ain't been to town, so no one will think nothin' of ya."

"That's good," said Frank, careful to avoid another gaffe.

Jesse continued, "Frank, you git up to the window and tell the teller you're there fer money alone and he ain't got to be afraid if he does what you say. Russell, you go back to the president's office. Go right in and git the drop on 'em. Tell 'em he either opens the vault or gits blown to kingdom come. And make sure the back door is unlocked. Soon as the vault's open, tie and gag both bank men." Frank and Russell nodded.

"Now," Jesse went on, "Reed, Cooper and me'll come in the back door with the bags. Straight to the vault, fill the bags, out the back door, all of us. Split up, two routes out of town and back here. Divide the bags, hightail it separate 'fore the sheriff even gits started. Questions?"

Only Frank spoke. "A good plan," he said, nodding toward Jesse. "Like you say, there ain't nothin better'n a careful thought-out plan."

"Okay," Jesse said, "we'll go over it agin' tomorrow and agin' on Thursday. Friday we do it." The men had grown increasingly restless during the idle time leading up to the heist. Now they were looking forward to the actual event. They recognized there was some element of risk, but they also had confidence in their leader and his carefully constructed plan. Friday could not come soon enough.

Albert Winter, the president of the Blue Springs Bank, began his day much the same as he usually did. He got up, shaved, got dressed, and went downstairs to have breakfast with his wife. He ate his usual two eggs over easy, one strip of bacon, two pieces of sourdough toast and one and one-half cups of coffee. During breakfast, his wife mentioned she wanted to take a drive in the country to see the turning leaves. Mr. Winter agreed to hire a buggy for Sunday afternoon and take such a drive. As he left the house he was in a pleasant mood and found the brisk temperature invigorating. He walked past the livery stable and turned onto the main street. He went by the sheriff's office, Perkins General Store, the post office, and the saloon. An odor of stale beer met him as he passed the saloon doors. Just past the saloon, he met the teller and the two of them walked together to the bank.

Mr. Winter unlocked the bank doors at five minutes past eight, which in his mind was close enough to eight o'clock. There were no customers waiting, and the bank would be open several minutes before the large clock on the wall inside read eight o'clock. He turned the sign on the door from "closed" to "open" while the teller raised the window shades and went to unlock the rear door of the building. As the teller went to his assigned station, Albert Winter said, "A bit brisk this morning, eh Barker? One of these days we'll have to get a fire going in that old stove."

"Yes, sir," replied the teller, "we sure will."

The teller understood that Mr. Winter's use of the word 'we' meant the teller or the clerk would be tending the fire. The bank president went through the door to his office, looking forward to reviewing the ledger books to ascertain how much business the bank had done so far that month.

A few minutes later, two men entered the bank. The teller did not recognize them, but greeted them with a friendly, "Hello. Can I help you?" Frank nodded to the man, walked up to the teller's window, and delivered the message Jesse had scripted for him. Meanwhile, Russell walked quickly around the end of the teller cage toward the rear of the room and slipped quietly into the president's office. The teller received Frank's news with wide-eyed wonder and told himself he would do anything the stranger asked rather than face the consequence of disobeying a man with a gun pointed directly at his midsection. The bank president was equally interested in self-preservation, and within a few minutes of Frank and Russell entering the bank, the vault was unlocked and the huge door swung open.

Jesse, Reed and Cooper had been waiting behind the bank with five horses. As soon as they heard activity in the president's office, they entered the back door of the building and walked directly through the office to the main room of the bank. As they did so, they saw Frank and Russell enter the vault. "Let's be quick," Jesse said, "I'm on lookout."

Jesse remained outside the vault while Reed and Cooper followed Frank and Russell inside. "Git them bags filled," Jesse called to the other men, "time's a wastin'." He expected the men could fill the bags in about ten minutes. To his surprise, the four men exited the vault in less than two minutes.

"Jesse," Cooper said, "it ain't there."

"What?" Jesse said.

"It ain't there," Cooper repeated. "The payroll ain't in the vault. It just ain't in there."

Jesse's face fell, then began to turn red. He walked directly up to Albert Winter and faced the bank president, nose to nose. "Where is it?" Jesse demanded.

The bank president swallowed hard and said, "That man is right. It isn't here. The army got it yesterday."

Jesse spoke louder than a man who does not want his presence known should speak, "But it comes on Thursday and goes on Friday!" he nearly shouted at the bank president.

The banker was beginning to sweat. "I know that's the usual," he said meekly. "But the army wanted it early this month. And what the army wants the army gets." Then he added, "If you had come yesterday, it would have been here." He immediately felt silly for his last comment.

The men all looked toward Jesse. He was their leader; he was in charge; the next move was up to him. He thought for just a few seconds, and said, "Never come close to bein' caught for a payroll. Sure ain't get gonna get caught for nothin'." He turned to Russell and said, "Ain't you got these two tied yet?" Russell, shaken out of a state of disbelief, quickly went about tying and gagging the bank president and the teller. Then, with Jesse in the lead, the men left the bank, mounted their horses, and rode out of Blue Springs.

"Never!" Jesse said to himself as he rode past the edge of town. "Never! I never heard of nothin' like this! Never!" He was beyond upset, but perhaps less about the lost financial opportunity than about the fact that his carefully concocted plan had failed. He simply could not believe he had made such a mistake.

At nine o'clock Friday morning the bank clerk arrived for work. When he entered, it seemed the building was empty. Then he heard sounds from the president's office. He opened the door to the office and was shocked to see his boss and his coworker tied to two chairs with gags in their mouths. "I'll run and get the sheriff!" he said and started toward the door.

"Mppphh!" the clerk whined.

"Oh, right," the clerk said. "I'll untie you first." Both men were untied and the trio headed toward the front door of the bank. They met the guard coming in, in as few words as possible told him what had happened, and asked him to summon the sheriff. A few minutes later, the bank president and the teller were describing in detail what had taken place, while the sheriff listened carefully.

As they neared the end of their recounting of the attempted robbery, the sheriff interrupted. "Wait a minute," he said, addressing the bank president. "Did you say the army payroll was picked up yesterday?"

"That's what I told them," the banker said.

"But that's not true," the sheriff replied, "we just brought it over here yesterday afternoon." The teller and the clerk looked confused.

"That's right," the clerk said, "but is it really not in the vault?"

Albert Winter allowed himself a slight smile. "It is not," he said calmly, "but it is safe and will be delivered as usual to the army this afternoon."

The sheriff shook his head. "I don't git it," he said, "where the heck is it?"

The bank president motioned toward the left front corner of the room. "See those boxes marked bank records?" he asked. "Armed guards and all are a good idea," he said, "but sometimes it's good to have a backup just in case. You know, there really is nothing better than a carefully thought-out plan."

8

THE HERO

"Ethan," the woman called from the kitchen, "go see if your grandpa is here. Tell him dinner is nearly ready." Ethan didn't like being interrupted in the middle of a game, but he knew his mother wouldn't let him get by with ignoring her request. He paused the game, got up from the sofa, and went out the back door of the house. He expected his grandfather to be sitting in a high-backed rocker on the back porch, his customary spot when he came to visit. But the old man wasn't there. Ethan looked around the yard, saw no one, and went back into the house.

"He's not on the patio," Ethan told his mother. "Well then, go look for him," she replied. "He didn't disappear into thin air." Ethan hated it when his mother made nonsensical comments like that. "Disappear into thin air," he thought, "as if I thought he did." He went back outside and stepped off the porch. The sun was low in the sky, partially hidden by clouds, and there was a chill in the air. A gust of wind stirred the leaves lying on the ground and pushed Ethan's hair back from his face. He wished he had put a jacket on. He walked toward the rear of the yard, peering into the trees on the other side of the fence.

Then he heard a familiar sound, the squeak of the gate in the backyard fence.

"Hello, young man," said Ethan's grandfather as he came through the gate. "What are you doing out on such a blustery evening?" "Looking for you," Ethan said. "Mom said to tell you dinner is ready." As the old man approached the youngster, he put a hand on his shoulder. "Thanks for letting me know," he said as a broad smile appeared on his face. "I appreciate the fact that you're not willing to let your grandpa starve." As the two began walking toward the house, Ethan looked up at his grandfather and asked, "What were you doing out on such a blustery evening?" The old man smiled again and replied, "Just visiting an old friend. Actually, a very special friend ..." His voice trailed off and he glanced back toward the fence.

As Ethan and his grandfather stepped up onto the porch, the boy posed a series of questions. "What kind of friend? And what makes him special? And where does he live? Can I go along to see him sometime?" The old man stopped walking. With a serious expression, he said, "First of all, he doesn't live because he's in the cemetery. And yes, you can go along to see him if you want to. As far as what makes him special, that will have to wait until later. We don't want your mother to call the police on us for being late to dinner, do we?" The boy smiled at his grandfather's attempt at humor, even though he didn't think it was very funny. As they entered the house, he wondered about the friend in the cemetery. He would ask grandpa to tell him all about it as soon as dinner was over.

Ethan liked the dinner his mother had made, for two reasons. First, because he really did like roast beef and mashed potatoes and peas. And second, because his younger sister didn't like peas, but their mother made her eat some anyway. His sister was OK, as far as sisters go, but he was still mad at her because of what she had done a couple of days prior. On the way home from school he had tried to jump his bike off the curb and crashed. His bike got a big scratch and Ethan's pants gained a hole in the knee. Not wanting to get in trouble, he had made up a story about some older kid pushing him over just to be mean. He didn't know at the time that his sister saw the incident, which she all too willingly described in detail to their mother.

After dinner Ethan had to finish two items of homework. Then he resumed the game he had been playing before his mother sent him to find his grandfather. He forgot about the conversation regarding his grandfather's special friend until he was getting into bed. He made a mental note to ask his grandfather about it the next time he saw him. When morning came, he was occupied with the normal routine of getting dressed, eating breakfast, and getting ready for school, so he didn't think about the prior evening's conversation with his grandpa. For the remainder of the week, the combination of schoolwork and activities with friends occupied Ethan to the point he seemed to have forgotten about his grandfather's special friend.

On Saturday, Ethan spent most of the morning playing with friends at the park. It wasn't until late morning, while riding his bike home, that he remembered his grandfather's promise to tell him about his special friend. Ethan was curious about who the friend was and what made him so special. His grandfather usually joined the family for Saturday lunch. Wanting confirmation that this Saturday would be no different, he went to find his mother. She was in the basement, digging through some old boxes. Ethan approached his mother and eagerly asked, "Is grandpa coming over today?" His mother tilted her head and, with a slight grin, said, "Well, good day, and I'm glad to see you, too. What's the excitement about your grandfather?" "Oh, just something he promised he'd tell me about,"

Ethan replied. "Well, he'll be here for lunch," his mother said, "and if he made a promise, I'm sure he'll keep it."

Ethan went upstairs, through the kitchen, and out the back door. To his surprise, his grandfather was sitting on the porch. "Oh, hi, Grandpa," he said. "Lunch isn't ready yet. Mom's in the basement." The old man smiled. "I stopped by early on purpose," he said. "I thought you might want to go along to see my special friend. It's just a short walk to the cemetery, and I'll tell you about him." Ethan was a bit uncertain about the idea of visiting someone in a cemetery. He was sure his friends would think it was weird. His grandfather, sensing Ethan's hesitation, reassured him. "You won't think it's so strange once we've been there," he said. "And I won't put an article in the newspaper for your friends to read about you visiting ghosts." Ethan half-smiled and thought, "Another one of Grandpa's corny comments." He nodded to the old man, and the two walked together to the gate at the rear of the yard.

There was a path just on the other side of the fence. The two walkers followed the path which after a short distance entered the woods. It emerged into a clearing about 100 yards later which abutted the cemetery. While they walked the old man began to tell Ethan about his special friend. "I knew him since we were boys," he began. "When I was your age he was my very best friend. And we stayed best friends all through high school." The grandson listened to the old man but said nothing. His grandfather continued, "But eventually he became more than my best friend," he said. "He was, and I guess he still is, my hero."

Ethan was surprised to hear the word hero, and it piqued his interest. He wondered if his grandpa was a hero too. For an instant he pictured his grandfather leading a group of soldiers in a ferocious battle, rushing forward and ... his thoughts were interrupted. "Do you have a hero, Ethan?" the old man asked.

Ethan thought for a bit and replied, "I'm not sure." His grandfather pursued the topic. "Well, do you know of any heroes?" he asked. Ethan frowned, then said, "I guess maybe we learned about some in school. Like George Washington. Or maybe Lewis and Clark?" The old man smiled. "Those might be, I suppose. But the man we're going to see was a different kind of hero." "Different how?" Ethan asked, becoming more and more interested in his grandfather's mysterious friend.

The duo entered the cemetery, and the old man led his grandson to a plot next to a large oak tree. The grandfather was silent as he pointed to a pair of granite gravestones. The boy read aloud the inscription on the first stone: Donald Charles Baker, January 17, 1921 – August 18, 2004. The boy looked up at his grandfather and asked, "Was he your friend?" "Maybe," the old man replied. "Now, read the other one." Ethan read aloud: Ronald George Baker, January 17, 1921 – June 16, 2009. The dates caught the boy's attention. "Hey," he said, "the birth dates are the same. They must have been twins!" The old man nodded. Then with a broad smile he looked down at the boy and said, "You're not so dumb after all." "Oh, boy," Ethan thought, "even in a cemetery, a corny joke."

"So, which one was your friend?" the boy asked. "I was friends with both of them. But Donald was my very special friend. He's the one who is my hero." "Was he in a war?" Ethan asked. "No, not a war," the grandfather said. The boy thought, then asked, "Did he run for president?" The old man shook his head. "No, he never ran for anything that I know of." Ethan scowled and tried again. "Was he a famous football player? Or baseball, or basketball, or soccer?" Again, the old man shook his head. "No, none of those," he said. "I know," the boy said with enthusiasm, "he was a famous scientist!" His grandfather chuckled. "Afraid not," he said. Ethan was growing impatient. "Well then," he said, "what *did* he do?"

"I'll tell you," the old man said. "But I need to start at the beginning. You listen and when I'm done, you'll understand why Donald is my hero." Ethan nodded and waited, and his grandfather continued. "When Donald and Ronald were born, their parents did not have much money. Their father had been injured in an accident and could only work part-time. Their mother cleaned houses and took in laundry, and they provided a stable home. Two years after the twins were born, they were joined by a sister, and a couple of years later by another brother. Somehow, the family always had a roof over their heads and enough to eat. And when the kids came to school their clothes, worn as they were, were always clean. The parents raised their children to be honest, thrifty, hardworking, and generous."

Ethan had been listening carefully. "So how does that make them heroes?" he asked. "Be patient. I'm coming to that," the old man said. "Donald and Ronald were both bright and did very well in school. They were both near the top of their class in high school, and their teachers were sure they would both do well in college. Donald was especially good in English, and wanted to be a teacher, or maybe even a professor. Ronald was strong in science, and decided he wanted to be a doctor. As they neared the end of their high school years, both boys had done so well they were accepted by big name universities." "Wow," Ethan said. "They were pretty brainy, huh?" "Yes, they were intelligent, and they studied hard," the old man said. "Everyone thought they would be very successful in college."

"So, what happened?" Ethan asked. The old man shook his head and said, "One evening at home, Donald overheard his parents talking about how they didn't have enough money to send both twins to college, even with the scholarships offered to them. So, after a good deal of thought, he decided to lie to his parents." "He lied?" Ethan interjected. "And he's your hero?" His grandfather chuckled. "Yup," he said, "the liar is my hero. He told his parents that he had changed his mind. He didn't want to be a teacher; he didn't want to go to college at all. He said he was tired of school and wanted to get a job and make some money."

"I get it," Ethan said. "He just said that because he knew they didn't have the money to send them both." "That's right," Grandpa replied. "And his parents were very disappointed. But they let him have his way. He never did go to college. But his twin brother did and became a fine doctor, too." "What happened after that?" Ethan asked. "What did your friend end up doing?" "After he graduated from high school, he went to work for a contractor building houses. He got married, bought one of the smaller houses his employer had built, and had several children. He worked hard and took good care of his family. But then the housing market crashed, and he lost his job building homes."

Ethan had been listening with rapt attention. "Did he have to give back the house?" he asked. "Not quite," his grandfather replied. "As it happened, Donald had overseen building a house for the president of the local bank. After the banker moved in, he found several small issues, which is not uncommon with a new house. The contractor's business was failing, and he refused to fix them. As the foreman on the job, Donald felt responsible, so he fixed them at his own expense. When he later fell behind in house payments, the banker remembered what Donald had done and did not foreclose on the house. Ah, that means he didn't take back the house."

"So did Donald sue the contractor?" Ethan asked. "My goodness," his grandfather said, "how did you learn to think like that? No, he didn't. In those days, most people were more likely to help each other than to sue each other." The old man paused a bit, then continued. "Donald found a job at the lumber yard and worked there for many years. Everyone liked him and trusted him, and folks often sought his advice on building projects. He was once offered a promotion to lumberyard manager, but he turned it down because it would have meant longer workdays and less time with his young children."

"But didn't he want more money?" Ethan asked. "I suppose he did," the old man answered. "In fact, when his kids got to high school he took a second part-time job to help pay for their college educations. He made sure every one of his kids got the opportunity he had given up to help his twin brother. And of course, that included the adopted ones, too." "Wait a minute," Ethan said. "What adopted ones?" His grandfather smiled. "Oh, didn't I mention that? Donald and his wife adopted two girls from ... I forget which country ... anyway, all their kids did well in school and graduated from college. Oh, except one, I forgot."

Ethan was intrigued. "What happened to that one?" he asked. "One of the boys went to some kind of acting school. I guess he was pretty good. He ended up in California, where he was in some well-known movies. He made a lot of money, but he didn't spend it all like some do. He gave a lot to charity, and I know he helped the homeless quite a bit. I think he retired from the movies now. Donald used to call him his hero kid." "That's kind of funny," said Ethan. "You called Donald your hero, and he called his kid his hero." The old man nodded and looked directly at his grandson. "You're right," he said, "maybe it takes a hero to raise a hero."

"So is that why you call Donald your hero?" Ethan asked. "Because his kids turned out OK?" The old man smiled again. "Oh, that and a dozen other things," he said. "I could tell you a lot more things he did, most of which simply came down to putting others first instead of himself. I hope that when you hear more about him you'll fully understand why he's been my hero all these years. And I hope you will decide to become that type of hero, too. Then I can call you my hero grandson. But right now we'd better get going. It's lunchtime, and we don't want your mother sending the police after us if we're late for lunch." The two of them turned away from the gravestones and headed toward the cemetery exit. As they began their walk home, Ethan thought, "I wonder if heroes make dumb jokes?"

9

THE ISLAND

It was the summer of '87, while I was on a hiking holiday in the North. An afternoon shower turned into a heavy rainstorm, and I sought shelter in a trailside pub. I was standing near the fireplace hoping soon to be warm and dry when some locals invited me to join them in a pint. I thanked them for the invitation, obtained a glass of ale from the bar and took a seat on the periphery of the group. I mostly just listened as the men discussed a variety of topics ranging from the weather ("Old Tom says his arthritis is worse again; we'll have rain on rain for sure") to politics and economics ("If them pols don't give an increase to we pensioners soon I'll have to limit my pub visits to every other day"). The latter comment drew a hearty round of laughter from the group.

The conversation gradually drifted from current topics to remembrances of past events and memories. A couple of the men recounted tales of travels at sea; one had apparently traveled more broadly than the rest. He described several faraway places he had visited, but one in particular piqued the group's interest. When he mentioned a place called Spon Island, an air of rapt attention settled on the group. All went quiet, men lowered their pints mid-sip, and a few eyebrows were raised.

It was evident I was about to hear something of much greater significance than the weather forecast or the cost of a pub visit. I ventured to enter into the conversation.

"I'm not familiar with Spon Island," I said, "but then I'm not from this area." Some of the men nodded and one of them muttered, "Hmmm, surely not." The man who had mentioned the island faintly smiled in my direction and said, "Understandable, for sure. Not a common port of call. It is a small island, well out to sea, filled with rolling hills and at one time a small mountain, now a lake. But not one to be easily forgotten once familiar." Some of the men raised their glasses and as in a toast offered a "Here, here" or "True, true." Then, silence. I realized the group was expecting me to prompt further conversation about the island. "So," I asked, "what makes this Spon Island so memorable?" The men reacted to my query by turning their chairs toward the man who had mentioned the island and adjusting themselves as if settling in to listen to a lengthy discourse.

"Ah," the man began, "what makes Spon Island so memorable? Answering that will take a little telling." Several of the men nodded, and one of them shot a knowing glance in my direction. The man upon whom we all directed out attention reached in his jacket pocket and extracted a pipe. He lightly tamped its contents with his thumb, then struck a wooden match on the underside of the table and held it to the pipe. After a few puffs to ensure it was well lit, he looked down the table at me and said, "There is only one Spon Island, and 'tis not what it used to be. But still, 'tis a place all its own and always will be." Though I was not sure what he meant by such a vague comment, I said nothing. The man apparently interpreted my silence as an invitation to continue speaking.

"Perhaps the most obvious thing that sets Spon Island apart from every other place is the name itself," he said. "S – P –

O – N describes the people that settled the island nearly five centuries ago. They were called Short People, Odd Numbers." At this, smiles appeared on some of the men's faces, while thoughtful frowns formed on others. The storyteller waited for my reaction. "Short people," I said, "how tall were they?" The man nodded. "I thought you'd wonder such," he said. "But short in stature they were not. Short in other ways they were." Again, smiles or frowns appeared on the listeners' faces. The man continued, clearly enjoying the opportunity to lead his audience along the path of what was to become a remarkable explanation.

"The people of Spon Island," he said, "were short of character. They were known to be short-tempered and short-sighted. They were short of patience and humility. And they were very short of any form of kindness and generosity. Ne'er was there a group of ruffians more unpleasant and miserable to be around than those who settled Spon Island." The man paused to allow his listeners to ponder this information and imagine the miserable state of affairs that must have existed on the island. "No one knows where the early islanders came from or how they got to be the way they were," he continued, "but uniformly despicable creatures they used to be, there be no doubt about that." He took a deep draw on his pipe and blew a cloud of smoke into the air. None of the men spoke, expecting the story to continue. I interrupted the silence.

"You said 'they used to be'," I said. "Have they disappeared? Is the island now uninhabited? And what about the Odd Numbers part of the island's name?" The man, grateful for my questions, used them as a springboard to launch into full storytelling mode, clearly intent on expounding on the subject of Spon Island without further interruption.

"You needn't worry about Spon Island going peopleless," he said. "If anything, 'tis a bit crowded with descendants of the early settlers. I did say "used to be" because truly they were the worst of the lot of mankind many years ago, but that was before the Big Change. That I will explain. But first, the little matter of Odd Numbers. That is in the name because those who settled Spon Island had a peculiar preference for odd numbers. Their houses all had an odd number of windows, the stairs had an odd number of steps, and the dimensions were always odd – like seventeen feet by twenty-three feet, rather than sixteen feet by twenty-four feet. If a family owned six cows, they would give one to someone that already had ten cows rather than own an even number. And enabling the other person to own eleven cows rather than ten was seen to benefit both families. Though they could not totally control such things, they strove to have an odd number of children and the women would try to hasten or delay delivery to give birth on an odd day of the month; ideally, the odd day of an odd month. All their children were given names with an odd number of letters, were given gifts only on their odd numbered birthdays, attended school through the seventh rather than the eighth grade, and well, you get the idea. They liked odds."

Without waiting for a response, the man continued. "So it was, according to what was passed down to later generations by word of mouth and later in written accounts, for about two hundred years. The Short People, Odd Numbers lived among themselves and followed their traditions. The few adventurous souls who visited Spon Island found some aspects of the culture interesting - the predilection toward odd numbers, for example - but the inhabitants were so singularly spiteful and unpleasant that none stayed long or ever returned. That is, until the Big Change." The man paused, awaiting the reaction that was sure to come. This time one of the other men at the table raised the obvious question. He raised his glass and took a sip, looked up and down the table, and asked, "What was the Big Change?"

"Sometime between one hundred eighty and two hundred years ago, when the people of Spon Island were going through an especially nasty time – it seemed everyone was always angry and jealous and selfish and cruel and proud – a lone visitor came to the island. No one saw him arrive and there was no foreign boat in the harbor. He simply appeared one day in the center of the village. The first person to see him was a man who, each day at about dawn, delivered milk to the residents' homes. He had just entered the village square, complaining aloud to his horse about the people whose house he had just left. He was telling the animal why he deserved the stately home on the north side of the square more than the family who lived there, when he saw a stranger standing in the middle of the road. The horse walked steadily toward the man as if it did not see him, but the man did not move. 'You stupid nag!' the milkman said, pulling the reins to stop the animal. He then cursed the man for being in his way but got no reply."

The attention of the men around the table did not wander. Their eyes remained on the storyteller, even as they occasionally raised a glass to their lips or groped in their pockets to light a pipe or cigarette. Even those who had heard the story before were transfixed, anxious to hear more about the stranger who visited Spon Island. The man continued the tale.

"The man was a bit unusual in appearance," he said. "Tall, thin, with long arms and a drawn face with deep-set, dark eyes. He wore a brown corduroy hat, a long grey overcoat over a black three-piece suit, and shiny black shoes with grey spats. He had a fresh flower in his lapel and a gold watch chain was draped across his midsection. As the milkman was observing the stranger, he heard the man say, 'The mayor. Or the governor of this island. Whoever is in charge, I must speak with him.'

The milkman, taken aback by both the commanding tone with which the stranger spoke and this abrupt request, acquiesced. 'I'll go right away," he said. "You wait here.' The milkman turned his horse and wagon around and left the square."

"Soon, the mayor of the village and every other resident had heard of the stranger's arrival, and the square was filled with people. The mayor approached the man and asked what he wanted. The man waved his arm toward the crowd and said, 'Alone, sir. We'll talk alone.' The mayor gestured for the stranger to follow him, and the two walked quickly to the mayor's home. There, the stranger did most of the talking. After a few minutes the two men returned to the square. The mayor gave a short speech to the townspeople, which he ended by saying, 'So there you have it, you ignorant bunch of fools. The vote will be held first thing tomorrow morning.' And the crowd disbursed."

The storyteller had obviously left out important details, and my curiosity caused me to again address the speaker. "What did the stranger tell the mayor, I wonder," I said. "And what was the vote about?" The interest of the other men at the table equaled my own, as evidenced by their rapt attention as the man at the head of the table responded to my question.

"The stranger – I won't speculate about his true nature or origin – the stranger had made a simple but dramatic proposition to the mayor of the village. He claimed to have certain powers or abilities or some such and could, if the people of the island wished, cast a sort of spell on the island. Over time the spell could erase all the profoundly negative aspects of the residents' character, changing the island to a place filled with kind, humble, patient, generous, caring people." I had not expected this answer to my question, and blurted out, "That's ridiculous! A charlatan, no doubt!" Even before I saw the expression on the other men's faces, I knew I had rudely misspoken.

"I'm sorry," I said, "that was uncalled for." "Perfectly all right," said the storyteller, "I had a similar reaction when first told about the stranger's proposal and the residents' vote." "Well, thank you for your tolerance," I said. "Oh, and what about the vote?" The man smiled and returned to his tale.

"The vote did take place the morning after the stranger's appearance," he said. "The mayor had explained that the stranger would only cast the spell if Spon Island's residents wished him to, so they voted. And the outcome was precisely the same as every other election recorded in the annals of the village. The vote was one hundred percent in favor and thirty-three percent opposed." Despite how strange the voting results sounded I held my tongue. "Then the entire village again gathered in the square and informed the stranger that the vote had carried. He stood before the crowd and told them the spell would come into effect the end of that day, and that they would have one responsibility if it was to be successful. Whenever a thought related to any of their shortcomings - whether anger or jealousy or selfishness or cruelty or pride – they had only to focus on the small mountain on the island – you remember I said the island had a small mountain and now a lake - and the negative thought would leave them. If they did this consistently, over time life on Spon Island would change from one of constant bickering, complaining and misery to one of warmth and pleasantry."

One of the men at the table, filled with curiosity, spoke rapidly as he asked the storyteller, "And what happened? Did they do what he said? And did it work?" The storyteller calmly answered. "Oh, yes," the man said, "they did precisely as suggested. And the spell worked, though the process was rather long and drawn out. It took years for the transformation of both the people and the island. But in the end, all was as promised. And the island continues today as it was at the time of the Big Change."

Some of the men nodded appreciatively, turned their chairs back toward the table, and raised their glasses to their lips. But one of them, his brow furrowed by a deep frown, remained facing toward the storyteller. After a few seconds, he said, "Didn't you say the island *had* a mountain? And if I'm not mistaken, did you perhaps say it now has a lake?" All eyes returned to the storyteller, and the glasses were returned to the table. The storyteller once again was the center of attention. "Very observant, sir," he said. "Permit me to address the final portion of the story of Spon Island."

"Perhaps you have observed that unpleasant people often walk about as if they were carrying something on their backs, whereas happier and kinder people tend to stand alert and upright, as if they are expecting something good to happen. And certainly, you have heard someone say they feel as if they are carrying the world on their shoulders, or when a problem is resolved, say they feel as if a load has been taken off them. These sayings are literally true and were doubly true for the people of Spon Island. When the spell took effect and they looked upon the island's small mountain, the weight of the negative thoughts that left their minds settled upon the mountain. And as time went on, the mountain bore heavier and heavier burdens of the anger and jealousy and selfishness and cruelty and pride from which the people were relieved. Eventually the weight of this was more than the mountain could withstand and it started to sink." The storyteller paused a few seconds for effect, then continued. "The mountain sank lower and lower and lower until it was level with the surrounding ground. And then it sank some more, until in the end, at the conclusion of the Big Change, it was just a huge hole in the ground. And when the rains came and filled the hole, it became a beautiful lake, which it is today."

"Well," I thought. "What a pleasant ending to a story with an unpleasant beginning." I pondered what I had heard, debating silently whether the man who told the story had devised it, or heard it from someone else, or even learned it as part of folklore passed down from generations prior. I decided to ask one final question. "Tell me," I said to the storyteller, "if I wanted to visit Spon Island, where is it located?" The man allowed a slight grin, then looked at me very seriously and replied, "The route itself is simple. But remember, I said it is a small island, so careful navigation is required. Sail north until you can go no farther, then go east until you feel compelled to reverse course and return. If you continue another day's sail, you will reach the islands of the Long People and the Even Number tribes. Put ashore there, present the natives with some useful gifts, and ask them to guide you to the island that looks as if it had a mountain but now has a lake. That is Spon Island."

10

THE LIEUTENANT

Lieutenant William Martin was in dire straits. He was behind enemy lines, separated from the rest of his squad and running low on provisions. He had no radio or other means of communicating his position to friendly forces, so a rescue mission was out of the question. Fighting his way back to his unit was impossible; his only armament was a standard officer's pistol. He had survived this long only by remaining hidden in a small area of woods, venturing beyond them to investigate his surroundings only under cover of darkness.

Some men if caught in such circumstances would conclude that their situation was entirely hopeless and simply wait in hiding until overrun by the enemy. But not Lieutenant William Martin. By persisting in his nightly reconnaissance forays he had discovered several things. First, the eastern end of the woods abutted a small farmyard from which he might be able to secure some food. The closest building to the woods was a barn, which held the possibility of some type of fowl, or a store of grain, or perhaps even a cow. Second, a small creek passed by the north edge of the woods, close enough to re-fill his canteen without alerting the nearby enemy. These two discoveries, he thought, might lengthen the time he could remain hidden in the woods.

The third discovery was of a distinctly different nature. A narrow road came from the west, then turned north and ran past the woods about fifty yards west of the edge of the trees. By keeping a careful watch on the road and analyzing the traffic upon it, the Lieutenant had concluded that some type of enemy encampment was located north of his position. More importantly, each day at about the same time a staff car drove slowly up the road toward the enemy's location. Lieutenant Martin was certain the car was that of a high-ranking officer, possibly even a general. This piece of intelligence prompted formation of an idea and then a plan in the Lieutenant's mind.

The plan constructed by Lieutenant Martin was of a type that occurs only in war. It involved unquestioning bravery, extraordinary risk, and a compelling commitment to inflict harm on the enemy. When carried out, the plan would at best result in the capture of Lieutenant William Martin, and more likely in his death. As a soldier, William Martin made a conscious decision to trade any prospect for escape from his hard circumstance for a chance to eliminate an enemy soldier of higher rank and importance than himself. He did not make this decision to achieve heroic status, but simply as a rational answer regarding the most effective use of one soldier in a specific situation. From that moment on, he focused solely on refining his plan, mentally rehearsing again and again every step, every element needed to ensure its successful completion.

If Lieutenant Martin had a rifle with a scope his plan would have been much simpler. He could have positioned himself in a spot with a clear view of the road, and when the staff car came up the road past the woods, played the role of a sniper. A single shot would mean the end for the enemy officer, and distance from the road might even provide a slight chance of escape before the origin of the bullet was ascertained. But William Martin was an officer, carrying only an officer's pistol. Therefore, his plan did not allow for the safety of distance.

Lieutenant Martin had not only repeatedly gone over the plan in his mind but had also, during the relative safety of dawn and dusk, physically rehearsed the movements of his plan. He practiced every step that would take him out of the denser part of the woods closer to the road, closer to being exposed to enemy sight, and just close enough to a passing car to shoot someone in the vehicle. He did not rehearse an escape plan; his proximity to the road in broad daylight would ensure he was spotted. The only remaining question was whether the enemy would take him captive or simply shoot him on sight.

Today was the day. Lieutenant William Martin had planned enough, prepared enough, and practiced enough. He had slept little during the night, kept awake not by fear or worry, but by anticipation and eagerness to finally act. He waited until mid-morning, then slowly, stealthily began moving through the woods toward the road. He went from tree to tree, pausing at each one to listen carefully and search for any movement ahead. At one point he heard voices coming from the farm-yard, but it was in the opposite direction from the road and he was not concerned. When he was about five yards from the western edge of the woods he knelt behind the trunk of a large tree and waited.

About half an hour later Lieutenant Martin heard a familiar sound. Faint at first, it gradually grew louder as a car ap-proached from the west. He heard it slow, then turn the corner to head north past the woods. He had imagined this so many times; he knew the car would pass directly in front of him in almost exactly two minutes. He slowly removed his pistol from its holster and leaned forward just enough to see around the tree. Then he realized he couldn't hear the car. He strained to listen more intently and barely heard an engine idle. The car had stopped.

The Lieutenant leaned around the tree, trying to get a glimpse of the car. He couldn't see it. What if it turned around? What if it drove up the lane to the farmyard? What if it didn't continue north, and he missed his chance? Just then, the car began to move again. It was coming north, not very fast, just like every other day. As it approached the woods the driver and his passenger were in clear view. The officer was on the side of the car closest to the woods. William Martin raised his pistol and slowly walked past the few remaining trees into the clearing beside the road. The car was now directly in front of him. He took a deep breath, slowly exhaled, aligned the sights of the pistol with the passenger's head, and squeezed the trigger. Bang!

Just then a voice called out from the barn at the other end of the woods. It was a woman's voice. "Billy, where are you?" the woman yelled. "Time for you to go get the mail. I just heard the mailman's car go by." "Aww, Mom," William answered. "Go on now," the woman said, "get the mail and bring it to the house. You can play with that cap gun later." "OK, Mom," William said, "I'm goin'." He put his pistol back in its holster, stepped out onto the road, and began walking toward the end of the farm's driveway.

11

THE PASSING

Samuel and Margaret Davies had been married nearly forty years when they acquired a young border collie they named King. The Davies had owned dogs their entire married life, both for companionship and practical help on their farm. They had lost their previous herding dog in an accident involving a passing lorry and depended on a good working dog. They bought the border collie from a breeder and trainer from whom they had purchased the dog it replaced. The new dog quickly adapted to the Davies herding methods and practices and proved an excellent choice for a herding dog.

The Davies' farm was of modest size, consisting of three small fields of cropland and a pasture which provided grazing for a herd of sheep. It was located a handful of miles east of Bedford, about thirty-five miles southwest of Cambridge. The land was good for farming, primarily flat, with a small knoll rising behind the farmhouse. The couple lived in what had been the carriage house of Pavenham Manor, a two-thousand-acre estate which fell into financial difficulties in the late 1940s. Largely due to the burden of postwar taxes, the estate was broken up, and the manor house was demolished in 1960. Samuel and Margaret Davies became the owners of a minor portion of the formerly grand estate. The carriage house was converted into a residence, a barn and a storage shed were added, and the Davies' farmstead was complete.

The border collie was a good choice and served its owner well. A predominantly one-person dog, King became the constant companion of Samuel Davies. Seldom was there a better match or closer loyalty between a canine and a human. Wherever he was on the farm, the dog was close by and seemed ready to help with the task at hand. The Land Rover never left the farmyard without King, and Samuel even fitted an extra seat for the dog on the tractor. Like any good sheep dog, it deftly herded the Davies' flock guided only by whistles and one-word commands from its master. Unlike most herding dogs, King could be trusted to move the sheep without human supervision, always in control of the herd but never overly aggressive.

The relationship between Samuel Davies and King became so well-known that people began referring to them as a single entity. A neighbor might be heard to say "Ah, there goes the Land Rover with Sam-n-dog, wonder where they're headed" or "Going to need a wee bit of help inoculatin' the lambs; think I'll ask Sam-n-dog for assistance." It was almost as if a new word – Sam-n-dog – had been added to the regional vocabulary. Even Margaret, Sam's wife, referred to the duo as a single entity, telling a neighbor, "Sam-n-dog is in the far north field this mornin'. Don't know when he'll be back."

Over time the bond between man and dog only grew stronger. The two learned to sense each other's moods and could communicate using only a few sounds and facial expressions. Some dog owners claim they can sense the animal's thoughts, or even that their pets can understand human speech. Samuel knew better than that, but sometimes the understanding between the man and his dog was uncanny. Perhaps it was just their constant companionship and the repetitive nature of their daily activities that made it seem like King truly understood his master's verbal instructions or observations.

The Davies' farm, like most smaller operations, kept the couple busy but still allowed for modest amounts of leisure time. In the evenings, from spring through fall when weather permitted, Samuel would often walk up the knoll behind the house, stand under the lone tree that stood at the crest of the hill, and survey the surrounding countryside. He would ponder the beauty of his surroundings, reflect on his good fortune, often sharing his thoughts aloud with his canine companion. King would, of course, never miss these outings, and many evenings it was the dog which reminded the man that daylight was fading and it was time to leave the house for their daily stroll.

Several years had gone by when, during an unusually cold winter, Samuel contracted a severe case of ague. King sensed all was not well and laid at the foot of his master's bed day and night. The dog ate little and lay with his head on his front paws, looking up only when his master's wife entered the room. Margaret cared for her husband as best she knew how, while also coping with the farm chores. She needed King's help with the sheep, but neither kind words nor scolding convinced the dog to leave his master. It was only when Samuel, awake and aware of what was happening, roused himself and said, "King, go with Maggie. Now!" that the dog reluctantly left the bedroom and accompanied his master's wife out into the farmyard.

When Samuel's illness did not improve it was necessary for him to be admitted to hospital in Cambridge. He was gone from home for five days, during which King continued his bedside vigil. When Samuel returned home the dog was overjoyed and welcomed his master with such enthusiasm that he had to be constrained lest his affectionate greeting knock the man to the floor. Samuel recuperated at home for another fortnight, the dog constantly at his side. The first evening the man felt well enough to leave the house the dog seemed to sense this milestone. It got his master's attention, went to the door and whined softly, a reminder that the knoll behind the house was waiting.

Samuel fully recovered, for which his wife and dog were grateful. The neighbors were glad to see Sam-n-dog active again. Many of them believed the dog had played a role in the man's recovery, and some even joked that Samuel's delight at returning home was attributable more to seeing his dog than to seeing his spouse. It was certainly not true, but an understandable jest given the uncommonly tight bond between the man and his dog. After Samuel's recovery, life went on as before. Man and dog spent their days together, often ending them by spending time together beneath the tree atop the knoll behind the house.

Having owned a number of dogs over the years, Samuel and Margaret were acutely aware of their limited lifespan. Each time they had lost a dog they had mourned its passing and then shortly gotten a new one. They knew that cycle would someday be repeated at the end of King's life. However, the closeness between Samuel and King meant that the inevitable demise of the dog would be especially distressing. The neighbors recognized it too, expressing their understanding of the situation with observations like "Aye, 'twill be a hard day when Sam-n-dog becomes just Sam, that for sure."

One morning, about a decade after Samuel's bout with ague, the couple were at the kitchen table sharing tea and biscuits when he said, "Ya know, Maggie, good ole King is not prone to live forever." His wife nodded. "Sad to say, you are right," she replied. "There's naught we can do 'bout that but be glad for 'im whilst he is here." The couple sat silently for some minutes. Then Samuel spoke. "I've noticed he must be becomin' a bit arthritic or such," he said. "It takes longer even to make the short walk up the knoll each evenin'. I know the day will come, Maggie, when he can't make it up the hill at all. And that will be the end, then." She responded, "That for sure, Sam. That for sure." Margaret rose and began to clear the table. Samuel went out of the house with King at his heels.

Over the ensuing months, Samuel and Margaret's conversation increasingly referred to the ultimate expiration of their beloved dog. The couple approached the subject with the pragmatism about mortality that stems from a lifetime of caring for farm animals, yet neither could think of King's eventual death in quite the same rational manner they faced the loss of a sheep or other animal. Try as they might to steel themselves against the day that was certain to come, the best they could do was continue bringing it to mind in the hope that doing so would somehow lessen the impact of the loss when it came.

It was a brisk fall morning, nearly a year later, that Samuel and King brought the herd of sheep from the farthest pasture to the one closest to the farmyard. The dog worked diligently as always, although he seemed to move slower than normal. His master watched carefully, alert for signs of illness or debility, but was not certain he detected any. For the rest of the day, dog and man went about their normal tasks together. At the end of the workday, the duo checked the sheep one more time, then went in the house for dinner. King had his usual dry food and water, followed by a treat that Margaret retrieved from a cookie jar on the kitchen counter. "Not good for 'im, Maggie" Samuel said with a frown. "That for sure," she replied, "but 'tis a small pleasure for 'im, and who knows how many more days he has to enjoy them." Samuel said nothing.

After dinner, the dog walked slowly to the door. He looked back at Samuel as if to suggest it was time for their evening walk up the hill but made no sound. "What, no whinin'?" asked Samuel. "Seems he's not quite right today. Per'aps he knows what you said, Maggie, and knows more than we about his end being in sight." Margaret sighed. "Some say dogs know of the impendin' death," she said. "If any dog would know such, this one would, that for sure." Samuel rose from his chair, went to the door, and led the dog outside.

Margaret looked out the kitchen window at the tree on top of the knoll behind the house. He saw the two of them, man and dog, standing together, apparently engaged in serious conversation. She smiled and said to herself, "Well, when the end comes, it will come with the two of 'em together. And that's the best we can hope for, that for sure."

Sometime later, Margaret glanced out the window again. The waning light of dusk allowed only a dim view of the tree atop the knoll. She knew Samuel and the dog should have been back to the house by now; they never stayed out until it was completely dark. She feared that King had either not made it up the hill or had so exerted himself on the climb that he might not come back down. And she didn't want Samuel to face that alone, so she wiped her hands on a towel, went out the door and around the house, and started up the hill. Against the rising moon, she could just make out the outlines of her husband and the dog. Sam was lying in the grass under the tree, very still. King stood over the man, waiting for him to start breathing again. No doubt, if the dog had not been coaxed away from the scene atop the hill, he would have guarded his master's body until his own heart failed him. That for sure.

12

THE PEASANT

The field, finally ripe for harvest, was just a short distance from the village. At nearly ten hectares, it was the largest of the two parcels on which Oleksiy Petrenko and his wife depended for much of their meager existence. In the spring the field had been planted in wheat, a staple crop in the area. The couple's other, smaller parcel was seeded in barley. Rain had been unusually plentiful during the spring and early summer and the Petrenkos were cautiously optimistic about their crops. But in early July a storm brought strong winds and hail, ruining the prospects for a bountiful harvest.

The Petrenkos accepted the damage to their crops with the same stoicism with which they had faced many other misfortunes during the nearly four decades they had farmed their two parcels of land. Oleksiy had reminded his wife, whose occasional tendency to complain about their circumstances did not meet his approval, that they ought to be grateful for even the reduced crop they were about to harvest. "Morichka," he said, "God does not owe us anything. Yes, he sent the hail, but he also sent the rain. If he had sent no rain, we would have nothing at all." His wife shrugged her shoulders but said nothing.

Like their neighbors, Oleksiy and Morichka lived in austere surroundings. They occupied a modest house in the village, behind which was a small barn that contained three animal stalls. Two of the stalls were empty; the couple's sole milk cow was kept in the third. Several chickens roamed freely in the yard. A tree stood next to the barn, its sprawling branches sheltering a small forge, a heavy work bench, and a stump that held an iron anvil. Oleksiy had taught himself the basic skills of wood and metal work, and he was often called upon to repair items for his neighbors and residents of the surrounding villages. This activity supplemented the meager income the Petrenkos earned from their two plots of farmland, only one of which was fully paid for.

The weather was hot and dry on the day Oleksiy began to harvest his wheat. He arose early and ate a small dish of boiled cabbage with a cup of weak coffee. His wife wrapped a small piece of sausage and two pieces of bread in a piece of thin cloth. This, together with a glass jar of water, she placed in a burlap bag. Oleksiy grasped the bag, nodded to his wife, and went out the door. He went behind the house, placed the waiting scythe on his shoulder, and began walking to the edge of the village and on toward the fields. He was, as always, look- ing forward to gleaning the ripened grain and safely storing it in the loft of the small barn behind the house. He soon found himself at the edge of his wheat field, where he placed the burlap bag in the shade of a large bush growing next to the road and commenced the harvest.

Oleksiy worked steadily and methodically throughout the day. He swung the scythe back and forth with a constant rhythm like that of a clock's pendulum. With each sweep of the blade more stalks of wheat fell, always aligned in the same direction. And each time the blade swung back Oleksiy took a small step forward, positioning the scythe for the next cut of the golden wheat. At intervals of about an hour, he interrupted the rhythm of the blade. He reached in his pocket and withdrew a small, flat stone which he used to hone the cutting edge of the scythe. Then he retrieved the jar of water from the burlap bag under the bush, took a few small sips of water, and returned to the task at hand.

When the glaring sun was directly overhead, Oleksiy laid down the scythe, walked to the bush that sheltered the burlap bag, and took out his lunch. He placed the small piece of sausage between the two pieces of bread and sitting partially in the shade of the bush, consumed the food. He wished there had been a tree large enough so he could rest a bit in full shade, but he would not have rested long anyway. After this brief respite, he again honed the cutting edge of the blade and resumed the back-and-forth sweep of the scythe. The sun was hot and there was no wind, but Oleksiy was content in the knowledge that he was at last harvesting the long-awaited crop.

About mid-afternoon, while pausing to sharpen the blade of his scythe, Oleksiy glanced toward the west and noticed two things: in the sky, a bank of clouds that suggested coming rain, and on the ground a cloud of dust that was growing as it came closer. The road beside the field was not well-traveled, and he was curious as to who had tasked a horse with carrying its rider on such a sweltering afternoon. His curiosity was soon satisfied when he was able to make out the outline of a coach pulled by four horses. As the unusual sight drew near, Oleksiy stopped swinging his scythe and stared at the conveyance. The coach, its gleaming woodwork accentuated by brightly painted scroll lines, was led by matched pairs of stately white horses. To his surprise, just as Oleksiy was about to resume swinging his scythe, the steeds slowed to a walk, then stopped. A man in uniform climbed down from beside the driver and walked into the field.

Oleksiy was perplexed. As the uniformed man approached, he set the scythe down and removed his cap. The stranger spoke first. "Good day," he said. "And to you," Oleksiy replied. "There's trouble with the coach," the man said. "A rear wheel is loose." Oleksiy said nothing. "Is there a blacksmith in the village up ahead?" the man asked. "Not a proper one," Oleksiy answered, "And not in the next village either." The man frowned. "Without a blacksmith how do the villagers get by?" he asked. "We fix our own things," Oleksiy said, and continued, "I have a small forge and help my neighbors and they help me. If I were not busy cutting my wheat I would offer to try to fix your coach, but as you can see the harvest is upon me and I must finish the field before the rains come."

The uniformed man scanned the field, then looked intently at Oleksiy. "Perhaps you are not aware of whose coach is in need of repair," he said. "Do you not know of Prince Vladislav?" Oleksiy's eyes widened slightly. "I have heard of the man," he replied, "as has everyone from here to the Black Sea. He is known to own much land in this area. But I have never seen him." The stranger nodded. "Well, my friend," he said, "it is his coach, his horses, and it is he himself sitting in the coach as we delay him by our conversation. Your help is needed, and I must insist that you accompany the coach to the village and see to its repair." Oleksiy glanced to the west at the growing cloud bank, then at the uniformed stranger. He took a deep breath, slowly let it out, then put his scythe on his shoulder and walked toward the coach.

The arrival in the village of an elegant coach pulled by matched teams of white horses did not go unnoticed. When the coach drew up next to the Petrenko's house, their neighbors emerged from their own houses, suddenly remembering things they needed to do in their yards or along the fences nearest the Petrenko property. As Oleksiy opened the door to his humble residence, Prince Vladislav emerged from the coach. He was a tall man, dressed in a white linen shirt with an embroidered collar, dark trousers, and tall, shiny black boots. His hair was grey, as was his full, well-groomed mustache. He stood erect, with his chin slightly elevated, as he surveyed the Petrenko property and its surroundings.

While the prince disembarked from his coach, Oleksiy opened the door to the house and called to his wife. "Monichka," he said, "come immediately. We have a guest." His wife responded from within the house, "What do you mean, a guest?" she asked. "And why are you home from the field so early?" Before Oleksiy could answer, Monichka appeared at the doorway. When she saw the coach, the uniformed man standing next to the horses, and the richly dressed man standing before her, Monichka was stunned. Her mouth opened but no sound came out, and she quickly covered it with her hand. The prince smiled slightly, held out his hand, and said, "My apologies for arriving uninvited." Monichka remained speechless.

Oleksiy broke the apparent spell under which his wife found herself. "This is Prince Vladislav," he explained. "His coach needs repair, which I have agreed to do. Invite him to our table and offer some food and drink." Monichka smiled weakly, then motioned for the prince to follow her into the house. She placed a plate, a bowl, a spoon and a glass on the table and motioned for her visitor to seat himself. She cut a large slab of bread and put it on the plate and filled the glass with home-made wine from a glass jug. She then brought a kettle to the table, and from it scooped a ladle of borscht into the bowl. The visitor had come on the day of the week when the Petrenkos allowed themselves the luxury of one meal of borscht, though there would be no borscht left for them this day. "I'm sorry we don't have anything like the strawberries from Leski," she said, immediately turning away in embarrassment for saying such a foolish thing.

The Prince ate his meal in silence. Then he said, "You are a good cook and generous. I thank you." Monichka nodded without smiling, and simply said, "You are welcome." She was thinking about the fact that the borscht she and her husband looked forward to each week had just been served to a stranger. She wondered whether Oleksiy was finding success in repairing the coach, and what he would say when he found out his weekly borscht was gone. Her thoughts were interrupted by the prince. "Again, thank you," he said. "I'm going to check on the repair to my coach." He bowed to Monichka, turned and went out the door. She sat down, shaking her head, relieved that he had left the house. She hoped the coach could be readily repaired and would soon be leaving the village.

Meanwhile, Oleksiy was having a conversation with the uniformed man who accompanied the prince. The man had not given his name, and Oleksiy had not asked. "So, what do you think, friend?" he asked. "I see you have fixed the wheel. Will it serve us well from here on?" Oleksiy nodded and replied, "Yes, I'm quite sure it will. But I looked the coach over carefully. The front wheels are fine, but the other rear wheel seems dry. It should come off and be greased lest it fail someplace along the road." The uniformed man frowned. "Well, better you fix it then we be delayed again," he said. Oleksiy nodded and began work on the other wheel. The uniformed man stood nearby and lit a cigarette. He did not offer one to Oleksiy, nor did he offer to help remove the wheel from the coach.

When the Prince approached the coach to inquire about the repairs, the uniformed man quickly put out his cigarette, moved closer to Oleksiy, and asked, "Is everything going all right? Do you need my assistance?" Before Oleksiy could reply, the prince spoke. "Was not the other wheel the one giving us trouble?" he asked. The uniformed man intercepted the question and explained to the prince that both rear wheels required attention. The prince took the news of the additional delay calmly but said nothing. He motioned for the uniformed man to join him in the shade of the tree next to the barn, and the two men visited quietly. Oleksiy continued to work diligently, and a short time later announced, "I am done. You should expect no more trouble from these wheels."

The prince smiled at Oleksiy, extended his hand, and said, "You have been a great help. I was sorry to interrupt your field work, and your wife has been a gracious hostess. Is there something I can do for you?" Oleksiy thought a few seconds, and said, "We have all we need. But may I ask, are you going on to the village of Lozove?" The prince looked at the uniformed man, who replied, "Yes, First Malynivka, then Lozove. We have land business there." "Why do you ask?" said the prince. "My wife has a sister there named Anichka Yvanova," replied Oleksiy. "Life is hard for her. Her husband died in the Crimean War and their only son left her for the monastery at Rozgirche. She writes that she is hungry much of the time." The prince pursed his lips. "I will look into it," he said. He shook Oleksiy's hand and climbed into the coach.

The prince's visit in the village had lasted nearly two hours, and Oleksiy and Monichka were glad the ordeal was over. Oleksiy was anxious to get back to the field and finish cutting his wheat. He picked up his scythe and began walking toward the gate. Just then, he felt the first drops of rain on his face. He looked to the west and saw dark clouds across the entire horizon. There was little point in going to the field. He would have to wait until tomorrow and would be lucky to be able to return to the field then. Judging from the sky, it appeared heavy rain was coming. It would then likely be several days before wheat harvest could resume, unless wind or hail accompanied the rain, in which case the remainder of the crop would be lost.

Several weeks later, Oleksiy was visiting with one of the neighbors who had observed Prince Vladislav's visit to the Petrenko's house. "And after you repaired the coach," the neighbor asked, "did the fellow pay you for your work? And did he pay you for the loss of crop he caused when he commanded you to leave off your harvesting?" Oleksiy shrugged his shoulders. "No," he replied, "we have not heard from him since he left the village that day. We thought perhaps he would come through again on his way back to his estate, but we did not see him." The neighbor scowled. "I'm not surprised," he said. "We struggle and they take advantage. It has always been that way." Oleksiy nodded. "What we can't change we can't change," he said. The other man agreed. The two conversed a bit more, then bade goodbye and parted. Oleksiy was sorry the man had asked about Prince Vladislav's visit as he did not enjoy being reminded of the incident.

It was after the first frost of autumn, when leaves are turning color and daylight hours are becoming noticeably shorter, that the Petrenkos received an unexpected visitor. They were seated at their table, preparing to have their usual modest lunch, when they heard a series of loud raps on the door. Oleksiy went to it, opened it, and stood face-to-face with the same uniformed man who had accompanied the prince on the eventful day of the past summer. "Oh, it is you," said Oleksiy, "what do you want? Are you broken down again?" He was not smiling, nor was the man in uniform.

"Who is it?" called Monichka. "Prince Vladislav's man," Oleksiy replied. "What?" Monichka exclaimed, "Are we to have bad fortune yet again?" The uniformed man stood motionless, with a pained expression on his face. "May I come in?" he asked. "We do not turn away anyone," said Oleksiy, "so we must also welcome you." The man slowly entered the room, averting his eyes from Monichka. "I have come to this village on the orders of the prince," he said, "and specifically for the purpose of delivering to you an important message." "Very well," said Oleksiy, "Sit and tell us what you must."

The uniformed man approached the table and sat in the chair farthest from Monichka, who continued to look at the man with a deep frown. "First to you," the stranger said, looking at Monichka. "The prince again thanks you for your hospitality and apologizes for the fact that an urgent matter caused him to travel without adequate preparation, thus finding it necessary to impose on you for food he fears may have deprived yourselves of needed nourishment." Monichka's frown softened somewhat. "The prince thanked me when he was here," she said. "He was not rude."

The uniformed man turned toward Oleksiy. "Now, another matter," he said. "The prince regrets that he was so distracted by the situation that caused his urgent travel that he neglected ... and he sincerely apologizes for this ... he neglected, after his promise to do so, to pursue the matter of your sister-in-law from Lozove." Now Oleksiy frowned. "Did the prince have you come all this way just to carry some apologies?" he asked. "I've not heard of such a thing." The man in uniform shook his head. "No," he said, "and now I must apologize for not bringing into the house the package I carried here."

The man arose and exited the house. Oleksiy and Monichka looked at each other without expression. The man soon returned carrying a flat package about thirty centimeters square, wrapped in brown paper. He sat down at the table and began to unwrap the package. "First," he said, "I must tell you something unpleasant. When the prince realized his oversight, he sent me back to Lozove to find Anichka Yvanova. Unfortunately, she died about two months ago." Monichka looked at the man in disbelief. "My sister is gone?" she asked. "Yes," said the man, "and the prince sends his condolences." A quiet moan escaped Monichka's lips. "So, as I thought, more misfortune. But if it is the Lord's will ..."

"Misfortune, indeed," said the man. "But there is also something that is definitely the opposite." As he said this, he finished unwrapping the package. Inside was a folder which he opened, revealing several official-looking papers. "I always carry papers like this in plain wrapping," he said. "There is less chance of being robbed on the road if their value is hidden." Oleksiy leaned forward slightly. "And these papers are of some value?" he asked. For the first time, the man in uniform smiled. "That they are," he said, "that they are indeed." Monichka, growing increasingly curious, faced the man and asked, "And you bring them here? To our village? To our house?" The man nodded.

"I must explain," the man said. "Prince Vladislav, in whose service I have been for nearly thirty years, is unmarried and has no heirs. He is no longer young and is quite aware that his days on earth are limited. Having spent much of his life expanding his holdings and accumulating considerable wealth, his attention has recently turned to the disposition of his estate upon his passing." "A good thing to consider," Oleksiy interjected, "He should have a will." "Oh, he does," said the man. "but he is not content to let death, shall we say, divorce him from the process of transferring his holdings to those still living." "I don't understand," said Monichka. "What has this to do with us?"

"An important question, indeed," the man replied. "Pardon me if I have confused you about the purpose of my visit, and please listen carefully to what I am about to say." Oleksiy and Monichka needed no encouragement to focus on the man's words. "The prince," he continued, "desires to use his wealth while still living to help those he sees as truly deserving of material blessings. When he encounters people whose lives have been hard but who have endured their trials with patience, faith, and perseverance, he urgently desires to contribute to their betterment. It is this urgency which inspired the trip that brought us through your village some months ago."

The man paused and withdrew a set of papers from the package on the table. He placed them in front of Oleksiy and Monichka, then continued. "There are three documents here. They are as of this day yours and yours alone. The first is a letter of credit from the prince in the amount of 10,000 karbovanets, upon which you may draw at any time. The second is verification that the mortgage on the field against which you have carried some debt has been fully paid. The third document is the deed to a fine field of 25 hectares that adjoins your farmland on the west side. All of this is yours compliments of Prince Vladislav and with his thanks for your kindness to him."

Oleksiy and Monichka stared at the man, trying to comprehend what they had just been told. Monichka turned to the man in uniform and asked, "But what did we do to deserve all of this? We have done nothing great or extraordinary in our whole lives." The man smiled and said, "Ah, but you have. Recall the characteristics I recited to you, the ones upon which the prince relies in distributing his wealth ... do you remember? The prince shares his wealth with those whose lives are built on patience, faith, and perseverance. In the prince's judgment, you deserve everything you are receiving. Now, if you will excuse me, I must be on my way. The prince is awaiting my return and will no doubt by now be anxious to send me on another errand."

The man stood, bowed, turned and left the Petrenko's house. Oleksiy and Monichka sat motionless at the table. Finally, Monichka spoke. "Would you like some boiled cabbage and bread?" she asked. "Yes, please," Oleksiy answered. Monichka rose and began putting the cabbage and bread on the table. "Tomorrow," she said, "tomorrow we will have borscht."

13

THE PREVARICATOR

When Robert James Wilson was born in a village in the English Midlands, he was not noticeably different from other newborns. His appearance was typical – wrinkly, somewhat pink, a disproportionately large head, and rather jerky movements. There was nothing unusual about his parents or other relatives or ancestors. His father, Jeremy Wilson, was immediately proud of little Robert, not knowing at the time that he would be an only child. His mother, Elizabeth Wilson – who for unknown reasons chose as her moniker her middle name plus the shortened version of her given name, thus identifying as Liz Mary – was a kind and understanding soul. She, of course, loved little Robert and cared for him as only a mother can, though some thought she doted on the boy to an excessive degree.

Prior to Robert's birth, Jeremy and Liz Mary Wilson had spent several weeks diligently acquiring the multiplicity of items needed to properly care for an infant. They rearranged their small house to make room for a crib, a rocking chair, and the stock of baby-related supplies they purchased. Within a few days after bringing Robert home from hospital, the Wilsons settled into the new routine of parenthood. Jeremy

Wilson, after just a few days leave, returned to his position as a clerk at an accounting firm, while Liz Mary assumed the role of stay-at-home mother. Both parents were delighted to respond to neighbors' inquiries regarding the addition to their family and presented little Robert to friends and relatives with just the right balance of pride and humility.

As he progressed from infant to toddler to a young lad, Bobby Wilson – his had mother insisted he would be called by his full given name, but she was unable to prevent others from effecting the inevitable transition from Robert James to Bobby – was in nearly all respects a typical English youngster. He formed friendships with schoolmates and other neighborhood children. He enjoyed reading, board games, and occasional hiking or bicycling outings with other boys. His parents, who were quite frugal, had put away enough money to send their son to public school. His scholastic performance, though clearly not remarkable, was deemed adequate by the headmaster and was satisfactory to his parents. Bobby participated in the school hiking club and played minor roles in several plays presented by the drama club. Perhaps the only area in which Bobby Wilson truly stood out as a student was his resolute interest in science fiction and fantasy literature. He dedicated countless hours to reading and eventually writing stories in the genre which he found so captivating.

Robert James Wilson's vivid imagination and tendency toward mixing fiction with fact began at an early age. As a young child he took a great deal of delight in inventing stories or other bits of fiction and insisting they were true. Nearly all children occasionally invent little tales and may even distort the truth to avoid punishment or simply to entertain themselves. Bobby's falsehoods went beyond that of a typical child. But because they were often inventive and unique, they were tolerated. In fact, his parents and others initially found them amusing, as they demonstrated a certain creativity on the youngster's part.

Neither Bobby Wilson's father nor his mother can recall precisely when they recognized that their son's behavior had become problematic. Like most parents, they knew that inventing tales was something most children did from time to time, but through parental guidance learned not to do so to an inappropriate degree. But young Bobby's penchant for spreading falsehoods went beyond the norm. And it seemed his tall tales were invented not just for amusement, but to satisfy a desire to see others believe a falsehood and act upon it.

When he was four years old, Bobby told two of his playmates that a middle-aged spinster in their neighborhood was a witch. He then convinced them that they must protect themselves from potential evil spells by wearing scrub buckets on their heads when passing by the woman's house. This prank was discovered only when one of the children neglected to return his mother's bucket to its normal place in the boy's home.

Before he was six years of age, Bobby invented his own version of the game "telephone" (this is often played by children sitting in a circle; a simple message is whispered around the circle, with the last child revealing a message considerably different from the original). Rather than passing a simple message between children, he initiated a rumor that a child in the neighborhood had a terrible, contagious disease. The rumor quickly passed from children to adults and resulted in several families self-quarantining. The local physician resolved the issue, but not before some children had missed several days of school.

Liz Mary Wilson, describing the issue to a close friend, said, "I don't know what we're to do. At first, we thought it was cute when little Robert made up stories and told fanciful tales. But he's older now and he does it so regularly one wonders where it will all end. And of course we don't want our Robert to be thought a liar." Jeremy Wilson put it differently. "The lad has got to realize that telling a bit of a fib is as far as it goes. Every child does that, at least until found out. But go beyond that, and one ruins one's reputation. It simply won't do. He's got to come around and stop this foolishness."

But young Bobby was not thinking about his future reputation and he rather enjoyed the attention his antics brought him. In primary school he found that teachers and administrators were as susceptible as their students to certain types of falsehoods, which broadened the audience for his antics. During his second year of school he convinced a classmate that the ponytail of the girl sitting in front of him was artificial and could be removed by a sharp pull. The gullible boy tested the idea with the expected result but was not successful in transferring the blame for the incident to Bobby.

A short time later Bobby managed to convince his teacher to exempt him from some of the homework assigned to his class. The reasonable justification for this special treatment was that Bobby had limited time to attend to his studies due to the demands of caring for his invalid mother. A good deal of homework was avoided until the teacher happened to visit the local chemist to purchase some headache tablets (it is not known whether the need for the tablets was directly related to having Bobby in her class). The teacher was shocked when, upon giving her name to the chemist, the lady behind her introduced herself as Bobby Wilson's mother and said that she had been hoping to meet her son's teacher.

The victims involved in these shenanigans were not selected because of any antipathy on Bobby's part until his fifth year of school when he encountered a male teacher whom he disliked a good deal. Bobby clandestinely gained access to a typewriter in a school office and prepared a letter of resignation on the part of the unpopular teacher. What he did not know was that the school's headmaster had some misgivings about the teacher and upon reading the letter was about to accept the resignation with enthusiasm. The fraud was not discovered until the headmaster mentioned to the unfortunate victim that he hoped the man would find a suitable position elsewhere. The source of the bogus letter was never discovered.

By the time he entered secondary school Bobby's reputation as an inventor of tales and pranks was well known. Some of Bobby's schoolmates found his unique behavior entertaining and no doubt encouraged it, but both his parents and his schoolmasters sternly disapproved of his actions and saw them as a form of delinquency that required correction. Bobby's headmaster viewed the issue as a dilemma for the school. "It's a sticky wicket, I say," the headmaster told Bobby's parents in a private meeting, "I don't want to question the lad's upbringing, or certainly his emotional well-being, but I and the faculty owe it to the other students to curtail this type of thing lest it erode the entire school's reputation."

Neither his parents' concern nor repeated cautions and lectures from the headmaster caused Bobby to deviate from his past pattern of behavior. Even the threat of being expelled did not deter him from inventing new tales and deceptions. In fact, his classmates were convinced that Bobby's periodic visits to the headmaster's office involved some type of academic recognition or encouragement toward advanced studies. Bobby even persuaded some boys in one of the lower forms that he met with the headmaster to tutor the man in a rare and difficult foreign language.

Throughout his school years Bobby steadily maintained that he was not, in fact, a person who lied. He consistently described his duplicity as "just making stuff up" and "interjecting a bit of fun" into the lives of those with whom he interacted.

When confronted by individuals affected by or upset about his actions, Bobby disregarded their complaints, apparently assuming they lacked a sense of humor. In a desperate attempt to change his behavior, his parents argued, cajoled, and pleaded with him. Jeremy Wilson even threatened to cease paying the fees for his public school, though Liz Mary would no doubt have objected to such a drastic measure. Every effort proved futile.

When Bobby entered sixth form, the headmaster tried a slightly different approach. He encouraged him to redirect his imagination by taking a creative writing class and becoming a member of the drama club. To the headmaster's surprise, the usually incorrigible student readily agreed to both. But shortly into his first term in the lower sixth, there was evidence suggesting that Bobby's behavior had not changed. Although no one admitted responsibility, someone associated with the drama club twice sent notices of play rehearsal cancellations to two student actors who had criticized Bobby. The second faux cancellation notice concerned the final dress rehearsal and necessitated a one-day delay in the play's opening.

The creative writing class initially went well. Bobby demonstrated ample creativity and writing ability and completed several assignments for which he received good marks. There was one incident involving mid-term exams, the results of which were posted just outside the instructor's office. On the morning grades were due the creative writing students queued at the appointed location to see their results and those of their peers. Several of the budding young authors were chagrined at their results, while others were ecstatic. Their emotions changed when about one hour later the authentic grade list was posted. Although the perpetrator of the hoax was not identified, Bobby Wilson was one of two students whose grades remained the same on both lists.

About halfway through the spring term several unexplained occurrences suggested that Bobby was continuing to apply his creativity in ways which were not constructive. An anonymous report of tainted food resulted in temporary closure of the dining hall, and the school's rugby team nearly lost their standing when an opposing team received a message, supposedly from the rugby coach at Bobby's school, stating that illness had struck several players and the team had no choice but to forfeit the match. The sham was discovered and the match was played, but not on the day originally scheduled. It was noted that the captain of the rugby team had quarreled with Bobby Wilson about the dining hall closure, but the rugby incident remained unsolved.

Despite his reputation and often antisocial behavior, Bobby's academic record was sufficient for him to continue to upper sixth form. His parents were both pleased that he had progressed academically as well he had and exceedingly anxious about the continued behavioral issues. They simply could not understand why their son persisted in such disruptive and pointless behavior. Did he not understand that once through school and responsible for his own livelihood, continuing his past conduct and attitude would almost certainly deny him the likelihood of keeping a steady job? Bright as he was, could he possibly believe that – in the cold, cruel world "out there" - his peers, his superiors, or his friends – if he had any – would tolerate continuance of such schoolboy antics?

Bobby continued to engage in disruptive pranks during his time in upper sixth, though it was never proven that he was responsible for them. No one knew for certain the source of the anonymous tip that led the police to storm the administration building to rescue the headmaster, reportedly being held hostage by armed intruders. One of the least-liked teachers suddenly became popular with students and faculty alike, due to a rumor of unknown origin that revealed that the teacher had won a considerable sum in the national lottery. Perhaps most mysterious were the identity and the methods of the person who convinced the BBC to send a news crew to the school campus to cover an impending visit by the head of state of a fictitious African country.

Throughout Bobby's school years his parents supported him both financially and otherwise despite all their frustrations and misgivings. He was, after all, Jeremy and Liz Mary's only child and a person of intelligence and a certain ambition. But as Bobby's graduation neared, the Wilsons' level of anxiety increased significantly. During the last couple of weeks of the school year, the headmaster called them in to discuss their son's future. They were not surprised by anything the educator said about their Bobby. They thanked the man for his patience and tolerance of their mischievous offspring.

After the meeting, on the drive home, Jeremy Wilson said to his wife, "Well, luv, some would say we shouldn't have let him go on so. That we should have cut off his school funding and let his stubborn self see where he'd end up. But he's our son and we've done what we think is right. He'll not have an easy time of it, of that I'm certain." Liz Mary was quiet for a time. Then she said, "Not unless he ... I don't know how to put it, exactly. It isn't that he needs to learn a better way, he surely knows as well as anyone the wrongness of what he does. I do so hope he gives up that part of him that causes such harm and hurt to others ... and eventually to himself."

They drove on silently for several miles. Then Liz Mary, not looking at her husband, said to no one in particular, "I suspect any caring person who knows our Bobby must worry about what will happen to him. Even people who don't know him, if they heard about the things he has done couldn't help but be concerned, could they? But all the caring in the world won't help if our Bobby won't change." Tears formed in Liz Mary's eyes and began to roll down her cheeks. She could not recall ever having felt so despondent.

Well, dear reader, do not despair. You need not worry one iota about Bobby Wilson's future, or about his parents. Because Bobby Wilson has no future. Let me say that again: Bobby Wilson has no future. But that fact is not going to cause any distress on the part of Jeremy or Liz Mary Wilson. And why not? Simple. At a public school in England there is a creative writing class. And in that creative writing class is a student who was tasked by his teacher to write a story -- a piece of fiction -- about a young person whose unruly behavior could not be readily explained. I am that student, and this is the story I wrote. THE END

14

THE RANCHER

His real name was Sam Harris, but everyone called him Tex. He was just over six feet tall, lean, and muscular, with a deeply tanned face accented by a bushy mustache. No one remembered seeing Tex wear anything other than square toe boots, long blue jeans, a shirt with snaps, and a black, pinched-front hat. On Sundays his jeans were pressed, and he switched to a grey cattleman hat. He truly looked the part of a Texas cowboy, which must have accounted for his nickname because he had never been to Texas. In fact, he had seldom ventured beyond his home state of Wyoming. He had twice attended the Denver Stock Show, and in recent years made cattle buying trips to Montana and western South Dakota. But he much preferred to be at home on his ranch.

Sam Harris had become a rancher the hard way. He began by working as a hired hand on a ranch in the central part of the state, where he was fortunate to have a boss who took an interest in him and taught him a great deal about ranching. The work was hard and the days were long. Summers were hot and dry and winters were often bitterly cold, but he liked working with horses and cattle, and he just couldn't see himself anywhere except outdoors. Years later, when reminiscing about his early ranching experiences, he said, "The ranching bug bit me, and I swelled up so bad I couldn't have worked inside a building."

It was Sam's boss, the ranch owner, who assigned him the moniker Tex. It happened on a Saturday evening when all the ranch hands had gone to town for a bit of well-earned recreation. The boss, who along with his hired hands had enjoyed several rounds of beverages in the local saloon, decided each man should have a nickname. The men did not object, since in the West it was common for men, especially for cowboys, to answer to a nickname. Since most of the names were short they added a bit of efficiency to communication on a ranch. More importantly, nicknames protected the men's privacy. It was not unusual for men to work together for years without asking or telling their full legal names.

The boss had a serious expression as he looked at the first cowboy. He frowned and pursed his lips as if deep in thought. Then he declared, "Everybody here knows you're the best bronc rider we got on the ranch. So that deserves some recognition." The other hands nodded in agreement and a few voiced their approval. The boss continued, "So, mister bronc buster, from now on you're Buster." The cowboy smiled and shook his head, knowing that his new name would follow him for a long time, perhaps for life.

The boss continued naming his crew. Each man received careful scrutiny, followed by a brief explanation of the rationale for the boss's choice and announcement of the man's nickname. In two instances, the cowboys avowed they already had nicknames. One, who wore a set of oversized silver spurs, said he had been known as Spurs at the ranch on which he previously worked. The men thought this made sense, and the boss confirmed that it would be the name by which the cowboy would be known.

Another man asserted that he had been known as Jinglebob as he sometimes wore a set of spurs that made a bell-like sound when shaken. But the boss vetoed the name. "I ain't havin' two men with names about spurs. Likely to call one of you and git the other. Since you're so proud of them jingly spurs, you're gonna be Showy." It was evident the hand was not overly fond of this nickname, and the announcement brought some chuckling from the other men. But the boss was the boss, so the man was Showy from that day on.

Nicknames were applied to each of the remaining employees. There was Dusty, Lariat (as one might imagine, a hand good at roping), Buckaroo, Longhorn (who really had lived in Texas), Cookie (who manned the chuckwagon), and Rodeo. Finally, the boss turned to Sam Harris. He looked Sam over carefully, then said, "Yup! You're the spittin' image of a Texas cowpoke if ever there was one. And whether you rode the range there or not, you're gonna be Tex." And that was that. The only person not christened with a new nickname was the boss. The ranch hands were aware he was referred to by townspeople as Mr. Hale, but it was not unusual for ranch hands to work for a man for an extended period of time without knowing or even wondering about his given name.

Because Sam was a hard worker, dependable, and a quick learner, his boss offered to help him get started ranching on his own. "Tell you what, Tex," the boss said, "I can't pay you any more than the other hands. But I'll let you use one end of the barn, and you take care of the calves that look sickly or are on the small side. The ones that make it you can have." Sam was grateful for the opportunity and showed his appreciation by working even harder on the ranch. Over a handful of years he was able to accumulate about thirty head of cattle, most of which showed no signs of having had a rough start in life. He was allowed to graze them with the other cattle on the ranch, though they were easily identified as separate from the main herd. Sam had registered the Lazy U, and his small herd carried that brand.

One evening after a long day of branding calves the boss pulled Sam aside. "Got an idea fer you, Tex." the man said. "The widow Morris's place is comin' up for sale. It's small, twelve hundred acres, but it's got water and you can lease a few sections of high country. It would be a good start fer you. I know you been savin' and I'll stake you two-thirds if you got the rest. Think it over." Then the boss turned on his heel and walked away, leaving his employee standing open-mouthed. Sam shook his head, looked up into the sky and murmured, "Well, thank you."

The life of a small independent rancher was far from easy. Money was scarce. Sam continued as a hired hand and tended his own herd during the few daylight hours remaining after a full day working on the boss's ranch. As his herd grew, he leased additional acreage, expanded the corrals, and put an addition on the barn at the old Morris place. The house was small and in need of repair, but he had other priorities and was not about to spend his limited time or money on improving it.

In order to grow his operation, Sam needed capital. As a very independent individual he did not relish the idea of borrowing money, but it was necessary. So he swallowed his pride and approached the local banker about a loan. He got the loan, though he did not appreciate the standard lecture the bank president gave to all the young ranchers who came to him for financing. "Now, Tex," the banker told him, "I'm putting this bank at risk giving you a loan with no more collateral than you're putting up. But I like to help the ranchers around here, and so long as you keep up your payments we'll get along just fine." He smiled a broad smile and shook Sam's hand. Sam thanked the man, left the bank, climbed up on his buckboard and started home.

One the way back to his ranch, Sam replayed in his mind the conversation with the banker. In his imagination he rewrote the script of their visit. "Now, Tex," he imagined the banker saying, picturing the man and his broad smile. "I'm going to loan you some money, not because I care about you, but because I'm going to charge you interest every day until you pay it back. And if you can't pay it back, just remember I've got a lien on your ranch. So even if you can't afford to eat three meals a day, you'd better pay me or the old Morris place will belong to the bank." Years later, recalling his dealings with the bank, Sam said, "I had what might be called a love/hate relationship with the banker. Except the love part was missing."

Despite his misgivings about borrowed capital and his dislike of the banker who loaned it to him, Sam made good use of the money. He expanded his herd, added new blood lines through the purchase of new bulls, and experimented with crossing two breeds of cattle as a means of improving the quality of his crop of calves. Each year he laid out a plan for herd expansion, additional pasture leases, and meticulous herd management and record keeping. And each year storms or drought, disease, or some other uncontrollable wreaked havoc with his carefully constructed plans. But through hard work, frugality, and the occasional help of friends, he slowly but steadily grew his ranching operation while keeping current on his payments to the bank.

Despite his steady schedule of hard work, Sam sometimes combined a Saturday trip to town for supplies with an evening of social activity. He would typically, if funds permitted, treat himself to supper at the café, then attend one of the public dances held at the schoolhouse. It was there that he became acquainted with Marie Johnson, the daughter of a prominent businessman in town. Marie liked the taciturn young rancher, his handsome appearance, and when it was expressed, his wry sense of humor. Their acquaintance became a friendship, and friendship gradually gave way to romance. Marie confided to her best friend that "I expect Tex will ask me to marry him, though he said very clearly that he won't take wife until he can provide for her. But he said he's got a good crop of calves, and when his yearlings are ready for market ... well, I think that's when he'll ask me." The friend asked, "What are yearlings?" "I don't know," Marie responded, "but I suppose I'll learn if I become Mrs. Tex Harris." Sam did not share his intentions with any of his friends, but his plan was in line with what Marie Johnson had told her best friend.

Two years later, Sam Harris asked the question for which Marie had been impatiently waiting. His proposal came with some caveats. "You know I'm a rancher," he said, "and I'll never be nothin' else. It ain't somethin' a person is likely to get rich at. You've been by the ranch, so you know the house is nothin' special. I'll do what I can to fix it up, but it ain't gonna be fancy." It was not the romantic speech she wished for, but Marie had decided long ago to accept. Her parents had some misgivings about her marrying a rancher, but they liked "Marie's Tex" and were supportive.

The couple married in late spring, after the branding was done, and Marie set about learning how to be a rancher's wife. She adapted better than many people expected. She did not shy away from physical labor, learned quickly, and was soon a capable and valued contributor to the Lazy U. She had promised her husband she would become a good ranch wife, but the reality of her doing so exceeded his expectations. Marie told a lady friend from town, "When I promised Tex I'd be a real ranch wife I don't know if he was sure I meant it. But I did, and I surprised him. And I even surprised myself at how much

I love the ranch, and the cows, and the horses, and everything about it!"

Marie and "her Tex" worked together day after day, month after month, year in and year out. Through good management, plain hard work, and a little luck, they succeeded in turning a profit more years than not. They lived frugally, made the mortgage payments on time, and reinvested any excess in expanding the ranch.

The couple had two children, a boy and a girl, whose education included the broad assortment of knowledge and skills required in ranching, and who learned to help with chores and other tasks from an early age. It seemed the whole family loved ranch life and simply lived for the Lazy U. But life on the ranch was not easy. Every season of every year brought challenges that had to be overcome.

At spring calving time they kept careful watch over the pregnant cows, taking turns checking them several times during the night. If a cow had a difficult birth, they both gave up sleep to pull the calf and ensure it was alert and able to nurse. During the long, hot summers, when the temperature could reach triple digits, they cut and stacked the prairie hay that grew in a meadow near the yard. Some years it simply refused to rain, and the couple watched helplessly as the green in the pastures faded away and the hills turned brown and dusty. Fortunately, their cattle were good foragers and tough, and survived by eking out just enough nutrition from sagebrush, mesquite, and some succulents. During the dry times Sam recalled with gratitude his former boss's suggestion that he purchase the old Morris ranch rather than some other place, because "it's got water."

In late summer and early autumn of the years when there was sufficient rain, Marie picked and canned garden vegetables and harvested apples from a half dozen trees she had planted her first year on the ranch. Autumn on the ranch was a time of beauty as various types of trees displayed brilliant reds, yellows, and oranges. Marie and Sam felt privileged to live in such an environment, though they had little time to bask in nature's splendor. The fall roundup, conducted with the help of neighbors for whom they returned the favor, was a particularly busy time. The cattle were gathered from the far reaches of the Lazy U, and those ready for market were sorted out and driven to the railroad terminus for shipment. It was the only time each year that the Lazy U was the recipient of cash income.

Winters were especially trying. As the leaves fell, the days grew shorter, and the temperature dropped, most of the herd came down from the remote hill pastures to the ranch yard voluntarily. But some did not, and any stray animals left in the high country might not survive the winter. Marie and Sam kept the children out of school for days, as the four of them spent every hour of daylight in the saddle, searching for strays and driving them home. Most years, they managed to get almost all the cattle down to the yard before winter hit.

The first snowfall was sometimes light and pretty, with large flakes drifting gently down to cover everything on the ranch with a soft whiteness. But snow season could also arrive with a sudden drop in temperature and a massive blast of wind from the northwest driving icy snow that stung the flesh and completely obscured from vision objects just a few feet from any person or animal caught in such a storm. As winter progressed, the chances of fierce blizzards lasting for days increased. Some years were worse than others, and as the spring thaw approached it was not uncommon to discover the carcasses of cattle that had stood with their backs to the howling wind until their nostrils froze over and they died of suffocation.

Sam often recalled that years before, his boss at the time had recommended he buy the old Morris place because "it has water." There were two water sources on the ranch. A wide stream came down from the hill country, passed through the Lazy U about a mile north of the ranch yard, and eventually joined Piney Creek. The stream was shallow, and usually by mid-December it was completely frozen. However, when the Morris family that founded the ranch had dug a well in the yard, they had the good fortune of striking an underground stream that produced an artesian well. Water from the well accumulated in a deep pond, and in the winter livestock could be watered by simply chopping holes in the ice on the pond. Sam tended to this every morning at the break of dawn so the cattle would not walk out on the pond ice. Once, he was tending to a sick cow and delayed chopping holes in the ice until an hour after sunup. A thirsty cow ventured out onto the ice, fell through, and drowned. He was never late again.

The worst part of winter, other than the possibility of severe illness or injury while snowbound, was the need to care for the livestock during a snowstorm or an extreme cold spell. Horses were kept in the barn, but the cattle were outside and there was always a chance of a cow going down during a blizzard, or a weaned calf wandering away from the main herd and foundering in the deep snow. Sam was more diligent than most cowmen in terms of regularly checking his cattle during inclement weather. He risked frostbite numerous times as he worked to keep his cattle safe and healthy, and one winter froze his feet sufficiently to require the amputation of a couple toes. The day after the doctor removed the toes Sam left the house as usual to check on the Lazy U's stock. Some might call such dedication foolish, but to Sam it was simply part of what a good rancher does.

As the operation grew Sam added one, then two, then three hired cowhands. He treated them well, taught them ranch and herd management like he had been taught, and expected them to work as hard and put in as many long hours as he did. The men liked and respected their boss, took better than average care of the livestock, and took pride in helping the ranch succeed. Over a period of years, the Lazy U became known as one of the largest and best run spreads in the state. It seemed that the years of sacrifice and commitment were finally paying off, and with just a couple more payments the ranch would be mortgage free.

Then came the spring that Sam hoped would never come. One morning, just as it was beginning to get light, he went out into the yard to check on some cows that had recently given birth. He noticed that two of the calves were not nursing. Instead, they were walking unsteadily, jerking their limbs and stumbling. As he watched the two newborns he felt a knot in the pit of his stomach. He walked over to the bunkhouse, roused one of the hired hands, and told him to ride to town and bring back the vet. He didn't check the remaining cows, but instead went into the house and waited. Later that morning the veterinarian confirmed what Sam already knew. His herd was struck by bovine virus. He had heard that the disease had been found a couple of hundred miles east of the ranch. He had no idea how it had traveled to the Lazy U. The vet said scientists were working on a vaccine that might be available someday. Until then, there was little he could do.

Everyone on the ranch seemed devastated. Marie and the children wept, and the hired hands very nearly did. Eventually, the neighbors would hear and send notes of support and consolation but would not come visit for fear of carrying the disease to their own herds. Sam said little. He patted the children's heads, whispered something to Marie, and went out into the yard. He saddled his horse and road off toward town. He wanted the banker to hear the news directly from him.

By the time the bovine virus had run its course, the Lazy U had lost nearly half its cattle and much of its reputation. What hurt Sam the most was having to tell two of the hired hands they would have to go. The disaster that had befallen the Harrises became the talk of the town. Citizens speculated about whether the family would leave the ranch voluntarily or wait until it was repossessed by the bank. Some merchants who had extended credit to Sam, assuming an inability to pay, debated whether to write off the accounts immediately or wait. A couple of prominent ranchers in the area wanted to offer Sam a job, but thought it prudent to wait until they knew when the Harris family was leaving the Lazy U.

Sam, meanwhile, was busy tending his remaining cattle, working the long hours he always had. In the evenings he sat at the desk near the fireplace and put pencil to paper. He added, subtracted, multiplied, divided. Then he repeated the process, revising the numbers as he went. When Marie stood by him and looked over his shoulder he waved her away, intent on finishing whatever he was working on. After several evenings of such activity, Marie finally became impatient. "Tex," she said, "I don't know what you're doing at that desk, but it's time you told me." Sam looked up at his wife, showed just the hint of a grin, and replied, "What I always do when I have a little time to do it. I'm working on next year's plan for the ranch." Marie was shocked. She sat down, put her hand to her chin, and shook her head side to side. "I don't understand," she said, "I just don't understand."

Sam rose, walked over to Marie, and put his hand on her shoulder. "Do you remember when I asked you to marry me? Do you remember what I said then?" he asked. Marie looked up at her husband. "Of course," she said, "about being a rancher and not getting rich and all that. Of course, I do." Sam smiled broadly. "Well," he said, "I meant what I said. I'm still a rancher, and we're not gettin' rich. But we're not quitin', either. We still have a heap more than when we started, and we're gonna do it agin'. And that's that."

Marie shook her head. "But Tex, what are we going to do for money? We'll still have mortgage payments coming due." Sam nodded. "I met with the bank president the day we learned the cows were sick. I had to listen to another lecture, but it was different this time. He said he 'most never had ranchers pay as regular as we do. He offered to carry the rest of the mortgage so we can get the herd built back up. And if we need a little more, he's Ok with that, too."

Thus began a period of years that resembled those when Marie and Sam were struggling to make the Lazy U a success. Although they were older now, the couple persevered with the same drive and devotion they had exhibited during the early years of the Lazy U. Slowly, steadily, through a course of ups and downs, Sam and Marie Harris again built their ranch into a noteworthy enterprise.

As in the preceding decades, years of rain were followed by drought, high cattle prices fell to money-losing levels, and season after season of vigorous and sometimes dangerous outdoor work took their toll. Sam lost part of two fingers of his left hand in a roping accident, suffered another bout of frostbite, and increasingly felt the effects of arthritis. His appearance, no longer that of a slender and handsome young man, would no longer have earned him the nickname Tex.

Sam and Marie's son remained on the ranch, hoping to take it over some day. He had been well schooled by his father, and there was no doubt he could manage the Lazy U. But, like many other next-generation ranchers, had no expectation that his father would let go of the reins any time soon. He eventually tired of waiting and went to work as a foreman on a large spread in Colorado. The Harrises' daughter fell in love with a young fellow whose father owned the local general store. She married and moved to town, leaving her parents disappointed and short a hand on the ranch. Sam did not think the move was permanent. "She was born to ranch," he observed. "She'll come back." But she never did.

Decades later, long after Marie and "her Tex" had recovered from the hard blows dealt them by cattle disease and drought and blizzards and myriad other challenges, after they had rebuilt the herd and the reputation of the Lazy U, after they faced the disappointment of their children leaving the ranch, an agricultural magazine published a series on notable ranches of the West. The editor selected the Lazy U as one of the ranches to be featured. Marie and Sam agreed, and a date was set for an interview to be used as a basis for the article.

One bright spring day a car drove in the lane and stopped, and a young woman got out. She approached the house and knocked on the door. Marie welcomed her into the house and offered coffee and cookies. Sam joined the two women and the Harrises sat in their front room answering the stranger's questions. Over the course of nearly four hours the woman questioned and prodded the couple, intent on gleaning all she could as material for her story. She made copious notes about the early days, the years when Sam and Marie worked so long and hard to develop the ranch, and how the Lazy U had grown to such prominence in the cattle business. She was amazed to hear about the trials, the struggles, the hard times the couple endured and the successful rebuilding of the Lazy U.

As the writer was concluding the lengthy interview, she thanked the couple for their patience. She then turned to Sam and said, "Tex, I have just one more question." Sam nodded. "Shoot," he replied. The woman looked searchingly at the man she had interviewed. "Looking back all those years and all the challenges you faced out here on the ranch," she said. "My

question is this: If you had not been a rancher, what occupation would you have chosen?" Sam tilted his head, smiled,
and said, "That's easy, ma'am. There's only one thing I've ever
wanted to be. It ain't easy, and it ain't somthin' you get rich at,
but it's what I am. I'm a rancher."

15

THE REUNION

The doorbell rang. Sarah Taylor glanced out the window and recognized the car parked in the driveway. She went to the door and opened it. "C'mon in stranger," she said with a smile. "I wondered when you'd make it over here to bring me up to date on the latest chit chat." The visitor entered the house, and without hesitation, walked across the room and sat down at the kitchen table.

"I think you've got that backward, Sarah," the woman said. "I'm not the one who spent last weekend in Kansas City. How was it, anyway?"

"You know," Sarah said, "it wasn't quite what I expected, but I'm glad we went. You'd be amazed at how much some people change in twenty-five years and how little others do."

"So how many showed up?" the visitor asked. "And did you recognize everybody? How about your old cheerleading foursome? Were they all there?"

"Whoa, Claire," Sarah said. "One thing at a time. First let me pour us some coffee. Do you want a brownie? I baked some for the kids."

"Coffee, yes please." Claire replied. "Brownie, no thanks. I'm sure they're good, but I'm trying to watch what I eat. But I'm sure they're good."

Sarah poured two cups of coffee and brought them to the table. Claire continued. "You'll never stop making treats for your kids, will you? I can just see you, when you're about eighty-five years old and your sixty-year-old son stops in, who by then weighs about four hundred pounds, and you insist he eat a plateful of goodies you just finished making for him and his sisters."

"Oh, Claire," Sarah said. "there's nothing wrong with baking something for your family. And you think we eat sweets all the time because that's what I offer when you stop in to visit. What do you think I should do, offer you coffee and a salad?"

"I'm just teasing," Claire said, shaking her head. "Anyway, tell me about the reunion."

"Well, you know," Sarah began. "Rob and I had only ever been to one other class reunion. That was our five-year. Then we moved, and between the cost of going back to Kansas City and not wanting to leave the kids we never went back. Then we got the invitation for this one and thought, 'Why not go? The kids are old enough to take care of themselves, and, you know, it's been twenty-five years since we graduated. It would be good to see our old classmates after all that time.' "

"I think it's great that you went," Claire said. "So, who changed the most? And how about your cheerleader gang?"

Sarah took a sip of coffee. "As far as changing, do you remember me telling you about a guy I dated named Brad Larson? You know, the captain of the basketball team?"

"I guess so," said Claire. "What about him?"

Sarah laughed. "Well, he used to be such a hunk. We had a reception before dinner the first night, and in walked Brad. Oh, my goodness. He's still tall, but that's about the only thing that hasn't changed about him. He's bald and he wears really thick glasses. And you just teased me about my kids gaining weight from my cooking. I swear, Brad Larson must weigh at least three hundred pounds, and most of it right around his middle."

"Wow!" Claire said, shaking her head. "Guess you're glad you ended up with Jim instead of him, huh?"

"That's for sure," Sarah answered. "It just proves you never know how people will end up looking. Or what they will do for a living. Like Allison Colter."

Claire frowned. "Who is Allison Colter again?" she asked.

"She was the tall one on our cheerleading squad," Sarah said. "You remember her, she's in the center of the picture I showed you before we went to the reunion."

"Oh, yeah," Claire said. "The tall one. The one you said was always kind of bossy. So, did she end up in some kind of unusual job?"

Sarah pursed her lips. "Not really that unusual, I guess. It's not so much the field she's in as the fact that she's on her own. She owns her own travel company. I think she said she has offices in six or seven cities and has plans for more."

"Travel, huh?" Claire said. "Did you tell her that you and Jim are always talking about traveling, and making plans for where you'll go after the kids are out of the house?"

"No," Sarah replied, "but I did tell her about where we live, and Jim's job, and the kids. She was amazed that anyone could raise four kids in a three-bedroom house. To be honest, Allison did most of the talking. But it was interesting. She's been all over. Her company arranges tours in Europe, Russia, Japan, even China."

"That's a little farther than you and Jim usually talk about," Claire remarked. "By the way, you two haven't given up your dreams of traveling, have you?"

"Oh, no," Sarah said. "we're just as excited about traveling as ever. It's just that we still have two kids to get through college. When they're through, we plan to buy a big camper and see the world. Well, not the world, but a good deal of the United States, and probably Canada."

Claire nodded. "Bet you'd love to go where Allison goes, though," she said. "You're always watching those travel documentaries on TV and talking about other countries. Don't you kind of wish you could change places with Allison, at least for a while?"

Sarah thought for a moment, then responded to Claire's question. "I have always wanted to visit other countries," she said. "To see the people, their customs, the cities, the countryside. I would love that."

Sarah sipped some coffee, sighed, put her cup down, and continued. "Don't get me wrong," she said, "I wouldn't trade my life with Jim and the kids for anything. But I do sometimes feel like I missed out on something I've always dreamed about."

Claire nodded but said nothing. Sarah picked up her coffee cup but did not drink from it. She said, "I guess the truth is I miss something I've wanted. And I wouldn't say I'm jealous of Allison Colter. I would just say she reminded me of what I've missed."

Just then the kitchen door opened and Sarah's husband entered the room.

"Oh, hi Claire," he said, breezily. "Just want to grab the car keys. Taking Riley to soccer practice. You know the drill; haul the kids, haul the kids. Gotta go! Say hi to Dan." And with that, he dashed out of the house.

"Oh, look at the time!" Claire said, "I've gotta dash too. Club meeting in fifteen minutes. Let's get together again soon. I want to hear about your other classmates and what has happened to them."

Sarah rose and walked Claire to the door. "Sure," she said. "let's do that. Maybe your place next time. Oh, and say hi to Dan."

"Will do," Claire called, as she got into her car. "And thanks for the coffee." As the vehicle backed out of the driveway, Sarah stood by the door, watching her friend leave. Then, she went to the kitchen sink, poured the rest of her coffee down the drain, and left the room.

In a city halfway across the country, in the twelfth-floor apartment of a glass-faced building, a mobile phone rang. The apartment resident picked it up and answered. "Hello?"

A voice on the other end of the call said, "Hey, it's me, Valerie. You got a minute? I just want to catch up after our little trip last weekend. Wasn't it something else?"

"Oh, hi Valerie," the phone's owner responded. "I'm just sitting here with a latte. Yes, it certainly was interesting. Hard to believe what happens to people you haven't seen for twenty-five years."

Valerie chuckled. "Well, somebody is probably saying the same thing about us. Like, can you believe how old Allison and Valerie look? Anyway, what do you think? Was it worth three days of your busy schedule to see your old comrades?"

"I'm not sorry I went," Allison said. "I have a lot to catch up on the next few days, but you know me. I'll put in whatever hours are needed to keep the expansion on track."

"I've no doubt about that," Valerie replied. "But I am curious. What's your takeaway from our weekend in Kansas City? Or should I go first?"

"Go ahead," said Allison.

"Well, I don't want to be catty," Valerie said, "and I really did enjoy seeing our old classmates again, or at least most of them. But when I think of some of them never really getting anyplace ... I mean, some of them live within just miles of where they grew up. It just, I don't know, it astounds me."

"I understand," Allison said. "There's nothing wrong with staying in one place, I guess. But it is limiting."

"That's an understatement," Valerie commented. "When I think of people like you -- hardworking, successful, always moving forward -- I can't imagine just staying where we grew up and doing whatever."

"Hmmm," Allison mused. "I guess it's all relative. Someone who lives on the Thames in London, or the Seine in Paris probably thinks you and I haven't gotten that far at all."

"Well, I know you're busy," Valerie said. "But I do want to know if you got to visit with the others in our cheerleading squad. I talked with Julia and Michelle but missed the others. Did you see them?"

Allison replied, "I didn't get to talk to Julia. I did talk with Sarah and her husband ... Tim or Jim ... and I spent a little time with Michelle. She's still very pretty."

"Julia lives in D.C." Valerie said. "She works in some congressman's office. She seems to like it. You said you talked to Sarah and her husband?"

"Yes, I did," Allison said. "They got married during college, I think. They have four kids, quite close together. They didn't leave our hometown until several years after school."

"Did you say four kids?" Valerie said. "Wow! That's a big family. I can't even imagine trying to cope with that. I'd need a nanny and a house big enough to get away from them, or else send them to boarding school."

"Now you're exaggerating," said Allison. "It's probably not as hard as managing all the people that report to you. They do live in a very small house, but she didn't complain about it. Besides, Sarah's kids are in college now; I think one or two have graduated. Her load will lighten up one of these days, and you and I will still have our noses to the grindstone."

Valerie laughed slightly. "Noses to the grindstone?" she said. "You make it sound like we're in a rock quarry or something. Don't forget, I've been to your suite of offices, and I didn't see any grindstones."

"I didn't mean it literally," Allison said. "I just mean that because Sarah's life is different from ours that doesn't mean she isn't happy or content. There's nothing wrong with living in a small house or having kids. My parents did that."

"Well, that was then, and this is now," Valerie replied. "I can't in my wildest imagination picture myself living in some small city, in a little house with a bunch of kids. If Sarah wants that, good for her. But I just can't see anyone doing that."

"That's because you're objecting to something you aren't suited for," Allison said. "That doesn't mean there is anything inherently wrong with Sarah's life. In fact, raising a family is a very worthwhile thing to do. The world needs people like Sarah."

"As Shakespeare said, methinks you protest too much," Valerie said. "Why are you so adamant about defending Sarah when you know she will never accomplish anything close to what you already have? And your future has never looked brighter! Next thing you'll be telling me you'd like to switch places with Sarah."

"I didn't say anything like that," Allison replied. "It's just that there is more than one way to define success. And being with Sarah in Kansas City reminded me that there are things in life, worthwhile things, that I don't have."

Valerie was silent.

Allison continued. "Don't get me wrong," she said, "I wouldn't trade my life for anything. But I do sometimes feel like I missed out on something. I certainly wouldn't say I'm jealous of Sarah Taylor. I would just say she reminded me of what I've missed."

"Hey, Allison," Valerie interjected. "I just noticed the time. I've got a staff meeting first thing in the morning I need to get ready for. Maybe we can touch base again in a few days and talk more about the reunion. I really want to hear what happened to your old boyfriend -- the tall guy that played basketball. OK? Gotta run!"

"OK, Val," Allison said. "We'll talk soon. Bye."

Allison put her phone down and went into the kitchen. She poured the rest of her latte down the drain. Then she walked over to the glass wall of her apartment. She gazed out over the city, lost in thought.

16

THE STORY

Jared Davis's mother opened the sliding door, stepped onto the patio, and called, "Time for cake!" She did not have to repeat the invitation. Almost before she could reenter the house a half dozen boys and girls crossed the backyard from the swing set, entered the dining room and scrambled onto the chairs. They sat looking toward the kitchen with expectant faces flushed from outdoor exercise.

Jared's mother soon entered the room carrying a round cake with seven lit candles. She placed the cake in front of Jared, who took a deep breath and pursed his lips to blow out the candles. "Just a minute," his mother said, "first let's everybody sing." She began the first phrase of the birthday song and the children around the table joined in with varying pitch, tempo and volume. As soon as the song ended Jared gave a hearty blow and the candles were extinguished. Mrs. Davis carried the cake to the kitchen and began to slice it.

Now," Jared's mother asked, "who wants ice cream with their cake?" She need not have raised the question, as all six youngsters immediately responded by yelling, "Me! Me!" Mrs. Davis smiled and proceeded to place slices of cake and large scoops of ice cream in soup bowls which she distributed among the young birthday celebrants. She had just placed a bowl in front of a girl at the end of the table when one of the boys asked, "Can we have seconds?" Jared's mother laughed and answered the boy. "Yes, you may," she said, "but not until everyone has their first one."

A short time later the bowls were empty, including the seconds. "Can I open my gifts now?" Jared asked. Before she answered, his mother cleared the dishes and removed the tablecloth to prevent the cake crumbs and drips of ice cream from contacting the presents. "Thank heaven for washing machines," she thought. With the table cleared, she said, "OK, kids, you can bring your presents to the table now." A flurry of activity followed, as the children rushed to get the gifts, each wanting theirs to be the first one opened.

The gift opening was done in the manner typical of seven-year-old boys. As each present was handed to Jared, he immediately attacked it with the objective of getting inside the package as quickly as possible. Carefully wrapped paper and bright bows were ripped from the package and discarded, after which the birthday boy reacted to the package's contents. "Wow, a Lego spaceship!" And a short time later, "Yeah! A video game!" followed by "Oh, boy! A remote-control truck!" These excited pronouncements continued as Jared opened his gifts, interspersed with his mother's reminders to thank the givers.

Jared's mother went around the room with a trash bag encouraging the children to fill it with the many scraps of wrapping paper. Then the six bundles of energy went back outside, anxious to try out Jared's new outdoor toys. They did not close the patio door, but Mrs. Davis decided she could monitor the children better with it open and left it that way. She was pleased, that except for the remote-control truck, Jared shared his new toys with his party guests. As the boys and girls were playing with the new toys Mrs. Davis's father entered the backyard. "Hi, Grandpa!" Jared called. "Did you bring me another present?"

Jared had forgotten that his grandfather had brought a present the day before. When Mrs. Davis's father responded to Jared's question by shaking his head "no" all the kids looked disappointed. "Have you forgotten the gift I gave you yesterday?" he asked. "Oh, yeah," Jared said, "but today is my birthday, won't you do something else?" The grandfather looked at Jared and asked, "What do you have in mind? Maybe a story?" Jared's face brightened. "Yeah, a story," he said, "tell us about Alaska. About all that exciting stuff you did there." Upon hearing her son's request, Mrs. Davis rolled her eyes but said nothing.

Jared's grandfather began walking toward the house and called over his shoulder, "You kids gather around over here on the patio and I'll tell you one of Jared's favorite Alaska stories." The youngsters ran to the house. Most of them reached the patio before Jared's grandfather did. He sat down in a padded chair surrounded by the children, cleared his throat, and began to speak. "Now kids," he said, "the story I'm going to tell you is not like the ones in your picture books or the ones you hear in school or in Sunday School. This story might have some scary parts, so just remember you're safe and sound here at Jared's house, you're not in Alaska." The children nodded to show they understood, though a couple of them looked a bit worried.

The opening caveat delivered, the man leaned back a bit in his chair and launched into his tale. "Well, kids," he began, "this all happened years ago, before any of you were born. I was a young man, big and strong, extraordinarily adventurous, and full of fortitude." He read the children's faces and realized some clarification was needed. "Extraordinarily adventurous and full of fortitude means I wasn't afraid of nothing," he said. Jared's mother called through the open patio door, "You mean you weren't afraid of anything." "That, too," her father responded.

"I first went to Alaska when I was about twice your age," said Jared's grandfather. The children's faces were blank. "I was fifteen," he said, "the same as Jared's sister Katie." His listeners' faces told him they understood. Jared's mother called from the house again. "Dad," she said, "try to stick to the truth, OK?" "I won't say anything that didn't happen or couldn't have happened," he said. Jared's mother sighed and thought, "Here we go again." She decided to let him entertain the children and deal with their questions later.

"As I was saying," Jared's grandfather continued, "I was fifteen years old when I went to Alaska." "Didn't you finish high school first?" asked one of the children, "Katie just started high school." Jared's grandfather smiled. "Oh," he said, "I finished high school at fourteen. I skipped a few grades because I already knew lots of stuff." Jared's mother called out from the house. "Dad!" Jared's grandfather knew what she meant, but just grinned and went on with his story.

"I left home with nothing but a rucksack - that's kind of like your backpacks – filled with some spare clothing, a few dollar bills, and some candy bars," he said. "I walked to the edge of town, out to the highway, and began hitchhiking north." "What's his hiking?" asked one of the girls. The old man smiled at her and said, "It's *hitch*hiking," he said. Then he noticed Jared's mother frowning at him through the open patio door. "Ah, that's when your friends, or probably their parents, give you a ride because you're not old enough to drive." His audience accepted the explanation. Jared's mother shot a warning look toward her father and returned to the kitchen.

"Anyway," the man continued, "it's thousands of miles to Alaska. It took me three months to get there. And when I did, winter had set in." "Is it cold there?" asked one of the boys. One of the girls asked, "Where did you live?" "One at a time," said Jared's grandfather. "Yes, it's cold. It's so cold in the winter there that everything freezes solid. Even the sunlight. It freezes so hard it can't move and it stays dark all winter." The children's eyes widened. The old man went on with his story.

"As to where I lived," he said, "I went as far as the road went, then I got a canoe and paddled up a river as far as it went. Then I got a dogsled – you kids would like that, it's a big snow sled pulled real fast by a bunch of dogs – and went as far as that could go. Then I walked about another hundred miles and got to the loneliest, coldest town in Alaska. And that's where I lived." The old man turned toward the patio door to see if his daughter was listening, but she was not in sight. He grinned again.

"What was the name of your town?" asked one of the children, looking up at the old man with a quizzical expression. "The town was just called The End," he replied. "Because it was at the end of as far as you could go. Any further and you would be at the North Pole." His audience seemed impressed with this information. "Did you see Santa?" asked another child. "Well, I'm not really sure," the man answered. "There was a man there – a big, fat, jolly guy that always wore a red suit – and he was always gone at Christmas. So it might have been Santa, but I never saw his sleigh or his elves, so I couldn't be sure."

The children were by now so captivated by the old man's story they probably would not have responded to an offer of additional cake and ice cream. He continued. "I didn't have much money, you know, so I had to build my own house. And to do that, I had to cut down trees and make them into logs and lumber. I cut every piece of wood all by myself." One of the boys asked, "Wasn't there a Home Depot?" Another said, ""Did you have a chainsaw?" The old man chuckled. "Oh, no," he said. "No chainsaw, no power tools, no Home Depot. All I had was an axe and a handsaw. It took a long, long time to build my cabin."

This prompted more questions from the storyteller's audience. "Was it hard?" "Did anybody help you?" "Did you get cold?" The old man shook his head. "No," he said, "there wasn't anybody nearby to help. And yes, it was hard work and it was terribly cold. Some days I had to start a fire to warm enough sunlight so I could see to work on my cabin." The children nodded, as they now knew about frozen sunlight. "After about half a year, my cabin was done and I had made some furniture – just a bed, a table, and a chair – so I had a place to live."

"Did you have a TV?" one of the children asked. "No, and it wouldn't have worked if I had one," the man replied. "Why not?" asked the child. "Because there was no electricity within a thousand miles," the man said. "There was no electricity, no running water, none of that stuff you kids take for granted." The children were not sure what "take for granted" meant but remained attentive. "No water?" one of them asked, "What did you drink? Milk?"

The old man frowned and shook his head. "Now where would I have gotten milk? Do you think I had a cow? Did I tell you when I hitchhiked to Alaska I brought along a cow?" The children realized milk was probably out of the question. Jared's grandfather continued, "What I did drink was water, but not from a faucet. There was a river close to my cabin. A river that came down out of the snowy mountains, full of cold, cold water. That's what I drank. But I had to go to the river to get it." The children pondered what they had heard. They tried to imagine a house with no electricity or water faucets. Most simply could not.

"Anyway, let's get on with the story," the man said. "I had lots of great adventures there, like the time .... "Why didn't you drink bottled water?" one of the children interjected, "My mom drinks bottled water." Another child answered the question. "Maybe there weren't any grocery stores." "That's right," the old man said, "there weren't any stores of any kind. All I had was what I got from the great outdoors." This prompted another question. "What did you eat?" asked another child. "If there wasn't a store, did you have to have your groceries delivered?"

"The only thing I had to eat," he said, "was what grew wild, like berries and such, and the wild game; there was lots of that." "What kind of games are wild?" asked one of the boys. "You mean like soccer?" The old man wondered if he was ever going to get to the truly adventurous part of his story. He decided to address the question regarding food, then use his answer to segue to a more exciting adventure. "Wild game means animals that aren't pets," he said. Most every day I would go hunting. I made my own bow and arrows and got pretty good at shooting them. I was never short of meat."

"What kind of meat did you have?" asked one of the children. "Oh, all kinds," said the man. "I had deer, fox, wolf, rabbit, lots of stuff." One of the girls looked shocked. "You killed a bunny?" she asked. The old man realized he had offended the sensibilities of his audience. "Oh, not a bunny," he explained. "Alaska rabbits are nothing like the ones here. They are big, as tall as a man, and they're mean, with big, sharp teeth. And they'll hunt you down and eat you like a lion or a tiger. So you have to kill them before they kill you." The children were duly impressed. The old man was pleased that his inventive description avoided an awkward situation.

"Anyway," said Jared's grandfather, "one day I went hunting way, far deep in the woods. I went probably ten miles and I kept seeing wolf tracks in the snow. I looked carefully at the wolf tracks and realized there were six or seven of them and they were following me. I knew they would attack me if they got a chance. So, here I was, all alone in the woods with nothing but my bow and arrow, and a whole pack of wolves after me." He paused to let the danger of the situation sink in.

"I had to outsmart 'em," he said, "so I began walking backwards. That way when they followed my tracks they would be going the wrong way. Then I climbed a tree and waited. Pretty soon here came the wolves, all mean looking and showing their big teeth, following my tracks. The biggest wolf – he was about the size of a small horse - was the leader. I drew my bow and took careful aim at the wolf. I knew if I shot the leader the others would run away and I could make it back home safely. But if I missed, the wolves would wait beneath the tree until I had to come down. And then they would attack me." He paused again.

"What happened?" asked one of the children. Jared's grandfather had a serious expression as he continued. "Just as I was about to release my arrow the branch I was on broke and down I went! But on the way down I managed to shoot the arrow. Just as I landed in the deep snow, it hit the lead wolf and he fell dead in the snow." None of the children questioned the feasibility of shooting a wolf while falling out of a tree. "Just as I had thought," the man said, "the other wolves gave up and left. I finished my hunt and went back to my cabin. Then I got another surprise."

One of the children asked the question the old man expected, "What kind of surprise?" Jared's grandfather responded, "While I was in the woods hunting it had snowed about ten feet at my cabin. It was all covered with snow, and it just looked like a giant snow pile without any doors or windows or anything." "What did you do?" a child asked. "Well, I was ready for big snowstorms," said the man, "and I had made a door on the roof of the cabin. So I just walked up a big snowdrift onto the roof. I dug down through the snow until I found the door in the roof, and I opened it. And I let myself down through the roof. If I hadn't been smart enough to think of that door in the roof, I'd have been stuck outside and might have froze to death."

A couple of the children shivered at the thought of freezing. One or two of the others appeared to be losing interest. The old man decided to intensify the danger aspect of his story. "But that was nothing compared to the biggest scare I ever had," he said. This renewed his audience's attention. "Yup," he said, "the biggest, baddest adventure I ever had up in Alaska was the time I was out hunting and ran right into a family of giant bears." He could tell from the children's reactions that they knew bears could be dangerous.

"I will never forget that day," the old man said. "It was spring, and it was warm enough that the sunshine melted and I could see pretty good. I was on the way back from a hunt, and I was carrying a big old elk – that's like a deer but bigger, with great big antlers. I had shot it with my bow and arrow. I was walking through the woods on the trail to my cabin. I came around a curve in the trail and there were four huge bears, right on the path. They must have smelled the elk I was carrying and were waiting for me." A couple of the children still showed signs of wavering attention so he offered a description of the bears.

"These were not ordinary bears like you see in the zoo," he said. "They were giant bears. They were taller than Jared's swing set, and wider than that storage shed over there." He gestured toward the other side of the yard. The children looked at the swing set, then at the shed, then back toward the story-teller. "Their paws were as big as a large pizza,"said Jared's grandpa. "Their claws were all sharp and as long as this." The old man held up his cane to illustrate. "And their teeth were like giant kitchen knives, as long as your arms." The children were mesmerized. One of them whispered, "Wow!" while a couple of the others shrunk back as if to distance themselves from the bears.

"So here I was," said Jared's grandfather, "face to face with four giant, hungry, growling bears. They stared at me, stood up on their back legs and roared – a roar so loud you could have heard it a mile away. And all I had was my bow and arrow and the elk on my back. If I didn't think of something quick, I would be their dinner." The children looked frightened. "What did you do?" several of them asked simultaneously.

"The first thing I did was grab hold of that elk by the antlers, swing it around over my head a couple of times, and threw it as far into the woods as I could," said the man. "I figured if they wanted food they might go eat the elk and leave me alone. They went a little way off the trail toward where the elk landed, just enough so I could sneak by them and head for my cabin. But when they saw I was getting away they turned around and came after me. I ran as fast as I could with the bears right behind me. They could run faster than I could, and by the time I got to my cabin they were so close I could feel their hot breath on the back of my neck." The children could almost feel the bears' breath, too. They could hardly wait for the old man to continue.

"So," Jared's grandfather said, "I just made it to my cabin as the bears caught up to me. I ran inside, slammed the door, and locked it. I pushed my furniture up against the door to help hold it shut and waited for the bears to give up and go away." "Did they?" asked one of the children. "No," said the man, "they wouldn't give up. They kept going around the cabin looking for a way to get me, and the longer they looked the madder they got. There was one window in the cabin, and one of the bears broke it and shoved a big paw – a paw almost as big as the window – inside, but he was way too big to crawl through the window."

"Then what?" asked one of the children. "Well," Jared's grandfather replied, "they just kept going around the cabin, pounding on it and roaring, and getting madder and madder. I thought about trying to escape by going up through the door in the roof and running away but I knew they would catch me. Then the worst thing ever happened!" "What was it?" the children asked nearly in unison, their eyes wide with anticipation.

Jared's grandfather looked straight at the children with an expression of near desperation. "They started pounding on the cabin door. All four of them. And every time they pounded on it little splinters of wood came flying off it. I knew they were going to break the door and get into the cabin. I grabbed my bow and my sharpest arrows and stood back away from the door. I put one arrow on the bowstring and pulled it back, ready to let it fly if a bear came through the door."

All of the children appeared to be genuinely frightened by the story, and it crossed the old man's mind that he could relieve the tension by smiling at the children. But he didn't smile. "Were you scared?" asked one of the children. "More scared than you are right now," he said, "but it don't help to be scared at a time like that. You just have to face the bears and fight 'em. So I stood there with my bow and arrow, ready to kill a bear before he could kill me. And just then there was a loud crash. The door broke into pieces and the first bear came roaring into the cabin."

"Did you shoot it?" asked a child. "I raised my bow and aimed that arrow right at his heart," the man replied. "But that bear's giant paw with those long, sharp claws came flying across in front of me and tore that bow and arrow out of my hand and sent it flying across the cabin. That big, ugly bear opened his giant mouth and I saw those huge teeth, and I smelled his bear breath as he grabbed me with his paws and shook me like a stuffed toy."

The children were in awe. One of them asked quietly, "Then what happened? What did you do?" The old man paused before answering. He took a deep breath and shook his head. "There really was nothing I could do," he said. "That bear had hold of me and there was no way I was going to get loose. I couldn't do a thing." There was silence for a few seconds. Then another child asked, "So what happened?" The old man looked the child in the eye and said, "The only thing that could happen. That bear ate me."

The children's jaws dropped and their eyes opened wide. They looked at Jared's grandfather as if he were a ghost. Then the old man broke into a broad smile, leaned back in his chair and burst into uproarious laughter. The children were confused. Still laughing, Jared's grandfather said, "Oh, did I fool you, huh? How could I be here talking to you if I was eaten by a bear?" One by one, the children's faces changed from puzzlement to enlightenment to wide, beaming grins. "Well, Jared," the man said, "Was that a good enough story?" His grandson smiled and shook his head. "It was the best one yet," he said. "Even if you had to lie a little."

17

THE TEACHER

Brad Stevens had wanted to be a teacher as long as he could remember. As a child, he often convinced his younger siblings to play school. Of course, he was the teacher, a role he relished and played with enthusiasm. Unlike many children whose career goals change multiple times, Brad never wavered in his desire to teach others. Thus, no one who knew him was surprised when following high school graduation, he enrolled in college as an education major.

After earning his degree, Brad found a teaching position in a large, urban school system in a neighboring state. He liked teaching and the students liked him. Unlike some teachers who see their positions as "just a job," Brad saw his as an opportunity to make the world a better place by inspiring his students to learn. Young people have the ability to discern which teachers really care about them, and as a result when students were asked to name their favorite teacher, many named Mr. Stevens.

Brad's dedication and success in the classroom was recognized by the district administration, and his principal encouraged him to further his education. By attending several years of summer school he earned his master's degree in school administration. He was soon offered the principalship of another school and he accepted. He was a good administrator and leader. He worked hard at communicating his vision for the school and building relationships with the staff and students.

With Brad as principal, the school's results and reputation improved, and after three years at the school he was appointed the principal of the largest high school in the district. He had a heavy workload and wide-ranging responsibilities but found the position fulfilling. He occasionally received offers of higher salaries from other school districts, but he never seriously considered them. His wife was teaching in a nearby district and their lifestyle did not demand a higher income. Both were happy and dedicated to their jobs and the years went by quickly.

Turning sixty was a bit of a wakeup call for Brad Stevens and his wife Becky. The milestone prompted a serious conversation about age, career, health, and eventual retirement. Although the couple both thoroughly enjoyed their work, they also recognized they were aging. And Becky, concerned about the hours and the stress involved in Brad's job, suggested he think about a way to somehow lighten his load. Over a period of several weeks and more discussion they decided it was time for a change.

As a successful, long-term school administrator, Brad had connections with many other teachers and administrators. He told a few of them of his desire to find a position in a smaller district and the word soon spread across the state. Within a few weeks he had corresponded with several smaller districts and met the school boards of three of them. He and Becky were familiar with all three communities, one of which was close to the city where Becky's parents lived. It was an easy decision for the couple and for the school board, which soon announced it had hired Mr. Brad Stevens as the new superintendent.

During the summer the Stevens moved to their new community, a town of about three thousand people. It was, as expected, a significant change from life in the city. Their house was smaller than their previous residence, but they agreed it was probably time to downsize. Becky almost immediately missed her fellow teachers and decided she would either sign up for substitute teaching in the elementary school or volunteer as a teacher's aide. Brad expected some challenges adjusting to the much smaller scale of the district's operation, but soon grew to appreciate the closer working relationships and lack of bureaucracy.

As superintendent Brad served the district's principals as both boss and mentor. He shared many of the methods that had proven successful in his prior district and modeled affection and concern for each student as a valued individual. The staff responded well to his leadership and parents began to comment on the school's impact on the attitudes of their children.

Of course, the positive atmosphere and outcomes of the school district were not solely due to the efforts of the new superintendent. Mr. Stevens had inherited a seasoned group of teachers, most of whom were effective in the classroom and liked by the students. Turnover in the district had been low and several teachers had been employed there for more than twenty years.

The first several months on the job, a good deal of Brad's time was consumed in learning about and forming relationships within the community. Experience had taught him the value of having connections with key people in his district. He got to know the mayor and city council members, pastors and priests, heads of local fraternal organizations, business leaders, and of course the school board and the PTA. He understood and appreciated the importance of support from these organizations and individuals, which was probably even more important in this smaller community. He was a busy man but felt less pressure than he had during the years he had worked in the larger district.

One of the positives a smaller school district offered was the opportunity to know each employee of the district. Brad enjoyed meeting and visiting with teachers, teachers' aides, custodians, cooks, bus drivers, and volunteers. He made it a point to remember their names and learn at least some details of their lives. He never passed an employee in the hall without recognizing them, and he often offered a word of encouragement or a compliment. He treated students similarly, though he could not call them all by name.

As part of his personal commitment to maintaining a good relationship with the district's faculty, Brad decided to review the personnel files of every teacher. One by one he reviewed their entire files and tried to remember key pieces of information. He read each person's annual evaluation form for every year, which in some cases meant reading twenty or more forms. Reviewing the files took many hours over a period of months. But Brad wanted to know about each person and to him it was worth the time invested. Sometimes, when he found something of particular interest, he would make a mental note to share the information with Becky when they were at home together.

Late one afternoon as he was reviewing the files of teachers in one of the elementary schools, Brad came across a curious bit of information. He had read the evaluation forms of one of the third-grade teachers, which were uniformly positive. The forms included comments like, "Has a unique ability to draw out shy or reserved students." "Gets problem students involved in creative learning activities." "Consistently receives high marks on parent surveys." Impressed by what he had read,

Brad checked the rest of the file. There was a note, dated a year earlier and signed by the prior superintendent, indicating the teacher intended to resign after two more years. She had been with the district for nineteen years and intended to retire after twenty years of employment.

Brad found all this interesting. But something else caused him to jot a note on a small sheet of scratch paper and put it in his shirt pocket. He then finished reviewing the file, closed it, and opened the next one. As with previous files, he read everything carefully and committed a few key facts to memory. When he had finished, he put the files back in the filing cabinet. He glanced at his desk and was pleased there were no evening meetings listed on today's calendar. He was looking forward to a quiet evening at home with Becky. He grabbed his briefcase, turned off the lights in his office, and headed home.

After dinner that evening Brad remembered the note he had put in his pocket. He took it out and said, "Becky, listen to this. I was going through employee files today and ran across something you will find interesting." She looked up from her reading. He continued, "There's a third-grade teacher – apparently a very good one – who has been with the district nearly twenty years." Becky looked quizzically at Brad and said, "And that's so interesting because?" "Because of something in her file," he said. "She graduated from the same small college you did – Western Teachers College -- and the same year." Becky put her book down. "Really," she said, "What's her name?" "Marla Johnson," Brad replied.

Becky frowned. "I don't remember her," she said. "Oh, you must," her husband replied. "Same small school, same major – elementary education – same year." "No, I don't," said Becky. "Maybe she got married and changed her name, but I don't remember Marla anybody." "Well," Brad said, "It was forty years ago. I guess I wouldn't remember all my classmates either."

Becky returned to her book. Brad picked up the newspaper and opened it.

Several months after Brad finished reviewing the elementary faculty files the third-grade teacher he had mentioned to Becky came to his attention again. He was going through a list of contracts up for renewal and noticed her name. "Marla Johnson," he said to himself. "Interesting. Looks like she's signing for one more year, just like that note in her file said she planned to do. Twenty years in the same classroom, then retirement. Not a bad way to end up." He wrote something on a sheet of paper, grabbed a paper clip, and fastened the paper to the list of contracts.

One of the practices Brad Stevens developed as superintendent was a brief one-on-one meeting with each teacher who signed their contract for the coming year. It gave him an opportunity to express appreciation for their service and for them to raise any issues or questions in a private setting. Like his review of every teacher's personnel file, this required Brad to invest time many administrators would not have spent, but he felt it was of value to both the teachers and to himself.

On the second Friday of May Brad's calendar included two one-on-one meetings with teachers who had renewed their contracts. The first was with a middle school math teacher; the second was with third grade teacher Marla Johnson. After school Brad met with the math teacher for just over half an hour, during which he learned of a minor middle school issue he would follow up on later. When he ushered the math teacher to the door he saw Marla Johnson waiting in the outer office. He smiled and invited her into his office. She returned his smile, walked in, and sat down in one of the chairs facing the superintendent's desk. Rather than sit behind his desk, Brad sat in the other chair in front of it.

Marla Johnson had been thinking about her one-on-one with the superintendent. Although she had made it clear a long time ago that the coming year was to be her last at the school, she was aware of her excellent reputation and knew good teachers were in short supply. "I'll bet Mr. Stevens is going to talk me into staying at least one more year or maybe two," she thought to herself. "But I'm not going to budge. I'm so looking forward to the things I plan to do when I retire. And one more year will give me enough points to max out the retirement schedule. So, one more year and that's it."

Brad sat observing the third-grade teacher. She seemed distracted or deep in thought. Then the teacher realized the superintendent was waiting to get her attention. "Sorry," she said, "I've just got something on my mind." "That's OK," Brad replied. He looked at the woman sitting next to him and thought, "Nineteen years. At about 20 kids per class, nearly 400 kids have had the opportunity to be taught by one of the best teachers in this school." He told her what he had just thought about, and she was obviously pleased. "I have truly loved every minute of my years here," she said. "But as you know, this next year is going to be my last."

Marla Johnson expected Brad to use her last statement as a segue to an attempt to convince her to reconsider her retirement plans. But instead, he asked her an unexpected question. "Marla," he asked, "do you know someone named Becky Defoe?" She thought for a few seconds, and said, "No, I don't think so. Does she live here in town?" "Yes, she does," Brad said. "but not under that name. She's Becky Stevens, my wife." Marla looked puzzled. She had no idea why the superintendent brought up his wife, let alone using her maiden name.

Then Brad asked another question. "Are you sure you didn't know my wife before I met her?" Now Marla was totally confused. She wondered where their conversation could possibly be heading. "No," she said. "I never knew any Becky Defoe." Brad nodded. "That's what I thought," he said. Marla frowned, and said, "Do you mind telling me why you're asking?" "I'm sorry for not getting straight to the point," Brad said. "I just wanted to be doubly sure." He adjusted his chair to directly face the teacher. "You see, Marla," he said, "my wife went to Western Teachers College. She majored in elementary education and graduated in 1981, the same year as you."

The teacher tilted her head to one side, smiled, and said, "I'm sorry I don't remember her. But after all, that was so many years ago. Maybe if I saw an old picture of her?"

Brad was surprised at Marla's response to his statements. He said, "I don't think that would make much difference. You see, my wife kept her old college annual. When I mentioned to her that you were a classmate of hers, she found her annual and we looked through it. There was no Marla Johnson in her class, in fact, no Marla anybody." The teacher's face went blank. She looked at the floor and put her hand to her mouth. For a full minute, no one said anything. When Marla raised her head to face Brad there were tears in her eyes.

Brad felt sorry for the teacher. But he had to get to the bottom of this. "Do you want to tell me?" he asked. "I don't know what to say," she began. "I completed three years of college. In another state, not at Western Teachers, but I quit school to get married. We had three children, and then my husband died. I was a widow without a job, and I was desperate. A friend heard about this opening for an elementary teacher. She told me to apply and say I had a teaching degree and said they probably wouldn't check with the school. And they didn't."

Marla paused. Her cheeks wet with tears, her eyes were red, and her shoulder drooped. Brad looked at her with pity, but not with surprise. He was virtually certain she had used some sort of ruse to get hired by the school district. Now he knew exactly what it was. Marla spoke softly, "So my secret is out. The worst is that one more year and no one would have ever known." Brad asked, "What will you tell people?" Marla sniffled. "The truth, I guess," she said. "It won't be easy."

Brad handed the teacher a tissue. She dried her eyes and nose, then said, "I'll hand in my resignation tomorrow. Unless you want me to do it right now. I can handwrite it, I guess." To her surprise, Brad asked, "Why would you do that?" "Because you found out," she replied, "it's the only thing I can do." "No, it's not," Brad replied. "There is one other thing you can do." The teacher was confused. "What's that?" she asked. Brad smiled at her. "You can hand in your signed contract and teach again next fall."

Marla was incredulous. "You don't want me to resign?" she asked. "Of course not," Brad said. Why would I want Marla Johnson, one of the best teachers in the district, to resign?" "But you found out I'm a fraud," she said. Her voice rose as she spoke. "You know I got this job by being totally dishonest, and now that you know you want to keep me? Why?" By the end of her question, Marla was nearly shouting, and Brad was thankful there was no one in the outer office.

"Look at it my way," Brad said. "I have a very good, effective, experienced, well-liked teacher who has done a great job for nineteen years. Why would I replace her with someone I'm not sure about just because that someone has a certain piece of paper?" Marla was astonished. "But my teaching certificate," she said, "It's invalid. I got it by lying." "Yes, you did," Brad said. "That's why there's one catch to this business of your continuing as a teacher in this district." Marla frowned. "What kind of catch?" she asked. "Just one thing," Brad said. "This has got to remain our little secret. You must never tell anyone and I surely won't either." With a weak voice, Marla simply said, "OK" and slowly walked out of the superintendent's office.

Thus, another twenty children in the third grade got the benefit of a year in a classroom with one of the best teachers in the school district. The following year Marla Johnson retired. She remained in the community as a respected retiree and volunteer and an active booster of the town's school system. But Brad Stevens did not keep his promise not to tell anybody about Marla's background. He shared the story with his wife Becky. And when he did, she simply said, "Who says educated people don't have any common sense? On the other hand, does it make any sense for a superintendent to risk his job and reputation like you did?" "I don't know," Brad replied. "Maybe I'm not as smart as some people. After all, I didn't attend Western Teachers College."

Mark Huenemann has been an educator, businessman, author, and consultant. He holds graduate degrees in business, education, and history, and previously published a collection of short stories titled Out West: Stories of the American Frontier.

Maple and Mister Universe

J.D. Pujals